Magic
and the
VENETIAN AMULET

GALE GENE

Brilliant Books Literary
137 Forest Park Lane Thomasville
North Carolina 27360 USA

CONTENTS

Dedicated To:
Pamela Taylor and Hal Lily

Joshua 10:25
Joshua said to them, "Do not be afraid;
do not be discouraged. Be strong and
courageous. This is what the Lord will do to
all the enemies you are going to fight."

PROLOGUE

In my first book, *Magic and the Terror at Loch Ness,* Paul Wonder, his father Noah, his Aunt Ruth, his grandma, and his dog, *Magic,* a giant golden retriever, went to Scotland on a filming expedition to which his father had been assigned. They planned to combine Noah's filming responsibility with a family vacation. Noah met up with his film crew, and Paul hooked up with the teenagers of the film crew adults because the film production crews were allowed to bring their own children on that particular film location.

Paul and his new friends, along with *Magic,* discovered many intriguing and haunted castles along with some horrors that lurked about in the Scottish highlands or mountains. *Magic,* Paul's dog, which mysteriously appeared one morning in Paul's bedroom when he was seven, became instrumental in fighting the evil forces that the teenagers encountered during their explorations. Together the teenagers, Jesse, Jeremiah, Adam, Delilah, Sarah, Anastasia and Paul, became the target of a troubled teenage boy, Judas, who had accompanied his dad on the same filming expedition. While Paul, *Magic* and the other teenagers were involved with exploring castles, monsters and whatever else was lurking about, Judas and his dog, Goliath, managed to follow and terrorize them. As the story unfolded, it became evident that Judas and Goliath were being influenced by some evil force. The confrontations were spectacular and supernatural. In the end, *Magic,* through divine intervention which gave her special abilities, was able to dispel the evil forces which had invaded Judas and Goliath.

Paul's Aunt Rue, a detective, was helpful in anticipating disasters even though the supernatural overtook her expectations as well as everyone involved. She had been an acting mom for Paul since his mom passed away when he was very young, No one expected to encounter a monster and have to engage in battles with the devil on this family adventure. Paul and his Aunt Rue worked closely to try and uncover the mysterious happenings in Scotland. Paul's dad, Noah, skeptical at first, realized that Paul was really on to something strange and curious that was going on with Judas and his dog. The whole family realized that ***Magic's*** name was appropriate as she proved to be very supernatural. Paul and Sarah, one of the other teenagers on the trip, were the only ones who saw ***Magic*** for who she truly was-a glowing lucky charm… a protective angel.

Paul and his father, Noah, developed a closer bond in the realization that God was there protecting them every step of the way, especially through ***Magic.***

Map of Italy

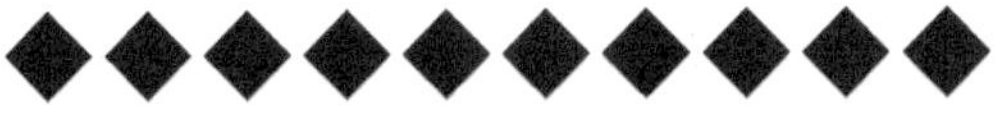

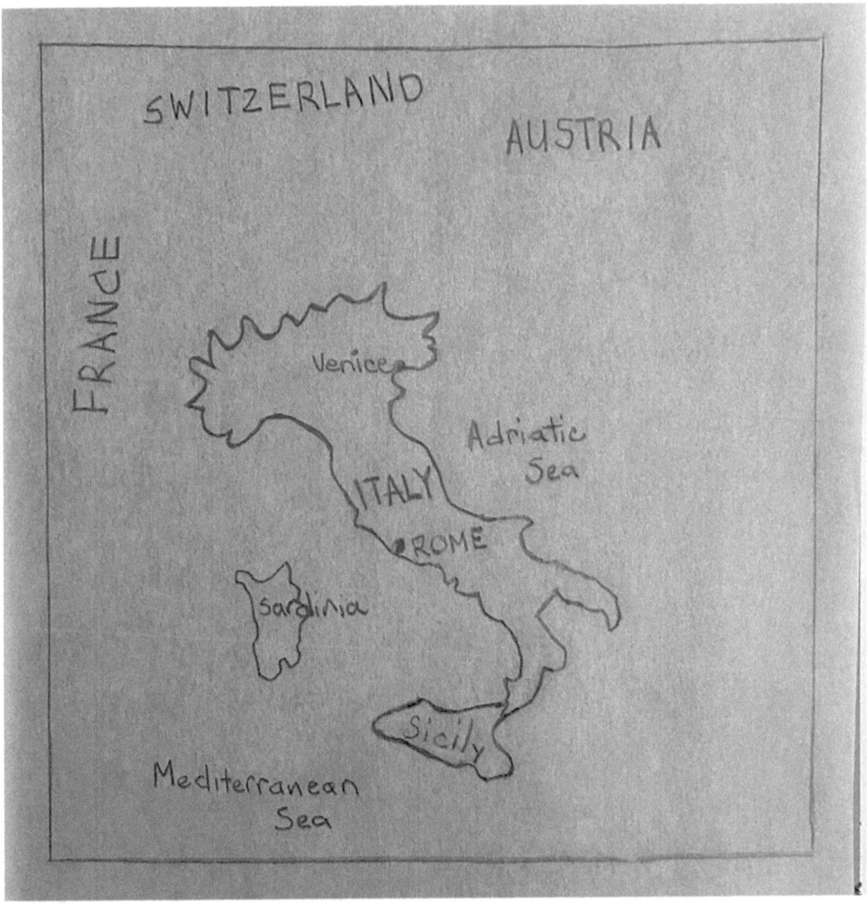
SWITZERLAND
AUSTRIA
FRANCE
Venice
Adriatic Sea
ITALY
ROME
Sardinia
Sicily
Mediterranean Sea

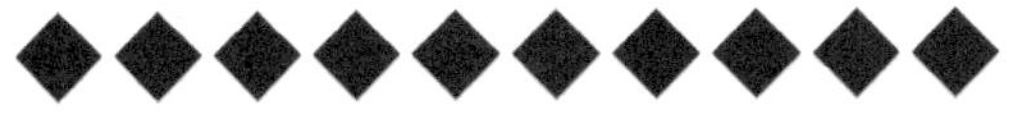

CHAPTER ONE
SOMEWHERE IN EGYPT

Horns are honking and motorcycles are screaming in the background. The smell of rotten food and decomposition permeates this part of the city as it is a garbage dump. The dirt roads are overflowing with stagnant water, and animals like cows, goats and dogs are living inside abandoned buildings and on the streets surviving off of the edible garbage. The people who live in this area are Coptic Christians, or Egyptian Christians.

"Why isn't Samson here?" questions Abel. "I made it perfectly clear that we were to all be here at 7:30 a.m. Did you forget to tell him? I wouldn't be surprised."

"No, no. I swear I told him to be here at 7:30," pleads Jonah, who's afraid of his own shadow. "He knows how important this is."

"Sorry I'm late," Samson says casually as his giant stature invades the dimly lit warehouse in Egypt. "You know how traffic is. This place is disgusting. Could you have picked a more out-of-the-way place with more of an infestation of the dregs of society?"

"Traffic… traffic. It's always something," complains Abel loudly over the noise of outside streets. "Stop complaining. As if you have anything to be a snob about. You're nothing but a thief. AND….That is the point…. no one would suspect us of anything gathering here in this dump." Abel is the brains of the operation and the only one who dares speak to Samson in this brusque manner. Most people cower in the presence of Samson, but not Abel. Samson is a Samoan who is huge, muscle bound and intensely serious. Abel's confidence comes from his brain power as he is a puny white guy. He knows that without his knowledge of Egypt and the museum, the caper would never have been formulated. If all goes well, everyone involved will owe him big time, so he thinks.

"So now that everyone is here, let's go over the plan," demands Abel. "Let's move back here farther so we can actually hear ourselves think." They all head to the bowels of the warehouse. "You all have your instructions and times. Tomorrow we will meet here to synchronize our watches. No one better be late, not even because of traffic. Leave two hours early, but get here on time. This can't fail. They are moving the treasures from Tut's tomb to Cairo soon, and, once there, the amulet will be inaccessible. It is now or never. The entire museum is under construction with this move, and security is lax. Stealing this amulet will be the pinnacle of my career! We will all be set for life, if we can pull this off. With possession of the amulet, our worries will be over, and we will have control of everything important."

Are you sure about the powers this so-called amulet possesses?" questions Samson. "Mummies are a creepy business."

"Of course I am. I have been researching it for years." replies Abel. "Whoever has the 'gold bird' will be able to access control like a god has."

"Yeah, yeah," agrees Jonah. "We'll be rich and able to do whatever we want. Of course, we will have to stick together, right Abel?"

"Sure…sure. Of course we will stick together." replies Abel.

"What assurance do we have that you won't take the amulet and run?" questions Thomas, who is another one of the five thieves who likes to whine and mistrusts everyone.

"Do you think I want to sleep with one eye open the rest of my life?" screams Abel. "Everyone has a part in this. None of us could do it alone. We need each other to pull this off and get away."

"Shut up both of you." shouts Samson. "We have discussed all this before. We will all get what we want and need and then be rid of this narcissist." Samson points to Abel.

"Yeah, who thought up the whole scheme?" sneers Abel. "Where would you idiots be without me?"

"Can we just move on and discuss tomorrow's plan," pleads Saul, another one of the thieves who is usually the quietest.

"All right, all right." says Abel. "Just stop arguing…. everyone. Here is what we will do once we are all here…….."

London, England, British Museum, mummies

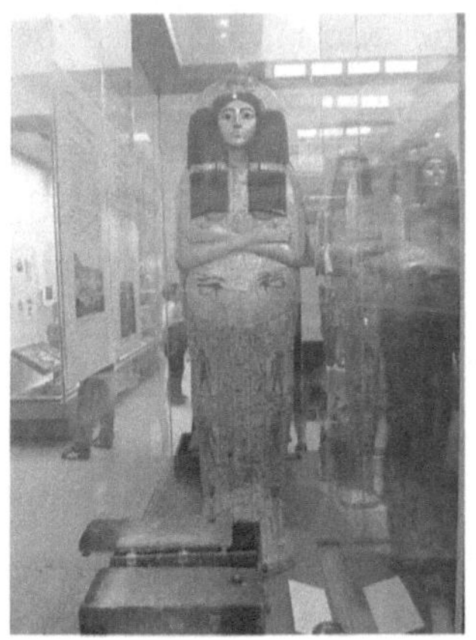

Chapter Two
Guess Who's Coming to Italy?

After our vacation in Scotland last summer, or nightmare in Scotland, as my dad likes to refer to it, we are planning another and, hopefully, less terrifying filming expedition. My dad was generous to take my Aunt Rue, my grandma, *Magic* and me along with him last summer on his travel documentary. This time Dad's director is sending the crew to Italy for another travel film. The whole encounter with the Loch Ness monster last summer in Scotland has had my family a bit on edge; all except *Magic,* my fearless dog. She is never upset, unless someone she is protecting is in danger. Since that mysterious trip to Scotland, my family will not go anywhere without our amazing *Magic*. She turned out to be quite the supernatural friend to have around on that trip.

My two best friends, Micah and Jacob, could hardly believe the whole story about how *Magic* fought Goliath, the devil dog of a kid, Judas. There were so many terrifying encounters with *Magic* and Goliath on the trip that Micah and Jacob were disappointed that they didn't get to go with us to Scotland. They had wanted to go, but my dad said that we were still all too young to turn loose in another country on our own. My dad is busy filming on the trips, so I have a lot of time on my hands, when I am invited to go along. My Aunt Rue watches out for me, when she comes along. My mom and I used to go on a lot of my dad's filming trips, until my mom passed away. Now my Aunt Rue, my dad's sister, lives with us, along with my grandma. This year Micah and I are fourteen, and Jacob is fifteen, so I think my dad might be considering taking all of us this time.

I call Micah and Jacob over to my house because I want to tell them my suspicions about the trip. My grandma and her friend, Phoebe, are making another awesome meal to serve at a wedding they're catering tonight. The theme for this wedding is Hawaiian, and it is going to take place at Venice Beach, right down the street from us. People like to have celebrations at Venice Beach because there are all kinds of interesting things happening there like muscle contests, artists painting and drawing on the boardwalk, roller skating, surfing, wake boarding, sand castle contests and many interesting characters wandering around. I think it is because it is the closest beach to Los Angeles, and a lot of different types of people live in Los Angeles. That means a Hawaiian feast for us because Grandma always makes enough food for Dad, Aunt Rue and me, and extra for anyone else who might be hanging around. Our house is like a constant party with good food and people.

"Man, does it smell amazing!" Exclaims Jacob as he comes through the screen door at the back of the house, which is the entrance to the kitchen. We have an old forest green craftsman style house made in the 50's. Our neighborhood has many different types of houses. That is the way it is in most beach communities in California. My friends always come around the back of the house and into the kitchen first. I think it is because they want to get in on the food action. Micah is right behind Jacob who has already seated himself at the table and is ready for some food.

"It smells like teriyaki," exclaims Micah. "Is it another Hawaiian feast?"

"You've got a good smeller there Micah." Replies Grandma as she's washing all the veggies at the sink with her giant colander. "You are right. It is teriyaki and another Hawaiian feast. Phoebe will be here in a few to help me with the finishing touches. I put a selection of ribs, chicken, pork and salads aside for all of you guys on the table." She motions to the long, wooden farmhouse table that seats eight people comfortably.

"Sounds like a luau. You're the best." Micah tells Grandma as he grabs a chair and folds his long, bulky body into the tall backed wooden chair. *Magic* barks her approval. "There you are girl," Micah says as he pets *Magic*.

"Paul," says Micah as he continues to play with *Magic*, "tell us about how *Magic* whooped that dog Goliath again. I love that story. I bet *Magic* does too."

Micah has been one of my best friends since second grade. Well, both Micah and Jacob have been my two best friends since second grade. We met at church and all love to surf, body surf, skateboard, and bike and do anything else that is exciting and challenging. Micah is the same age as me with dark hair and eyes, stocky and a little shorter than me. Jacob is one year older, blonde with blue eyes, taller than me and very stocky. We are all hyper, noisy, really annoying and inseparable but look totally different. I with my red hair and blue eyes are a contrast to Micah and Jacob. They always want to hear the stories of how *Magic* whopped Goliath's you-know-what last year on vacation in Scotland. The best part about the fights was that *Magic* always won. In the end, Goliath and Judas were saved by *Magic* and Devine intervention.

As my dad says, "God is always in charge."

"I'm thinking that my dad may be having second thoughts about taking us on the assignment he has in Italy," I tell Micah and Jacob.

"What do you mean?" asks Jacob. "Is he having second thoughts about taking us or second thoughts about taking you?"

"Taking us, you dummy," I respond laughing. "He was quizzing me last night with questions about whether your parents would consider letting you go with him to Europe. I am pretty sure he wants you guys to come"

"Honest?" questions Micah. "Dude! Do you know what this means? Are you kidding around, or are you serious?"

"No, I am not kidding around." I reassure Micah. "I think he is actually considering taking all of us. He thinks that we are used to doing things together and figuring out solutions to problems that arise or getting out of sticky situations. I don't know where he got that idea. I don't tell him about half the stuff that we get into and out of. I think Aunt Rue is more on to us than him."

"When is the trip?" questions Jacob.

"Next month, right after school's out." I reply. "He said he wanted to talk with me tonight. I think he may be considering calling your parents today to see if they are okay with it. I told him that you guys had your passports on account of that mission trip you two took to the Dominican Republic last year."

"I can't believe it!" exclaims Micah. "Are you messing with us, Paul?"

"No. I'm serious. That's why I called you over!" I exclaim "He hasn't confirmed that he was going to ask you guys, but he sure has been hinting around about it. I am pretty sure he wouldn't mention it, if he wasn't thinking seriously about it. You know how he is. He has to make sure everything is all in order before we can make any decisions."

"So just where is it that your dad is going?" questions Jacob.

"A bunch of places in Italy," I reply.

They all fist bump between bites. "Where in Italy?" asks Micah?"

"Well," I say, "I think we are starting in Rome and moving on to Venice and then I'm not really sure where esle."

"My parents better let me go," whines Jacob. "Do you think that kid, Judas with his dog Goliath, will be going? What about the other kids who were there. Do you keep in touch with them at all?"

"Nah," I reply, "I haven't heard anything about them, but, if my dad gets to take me and possibly you guys, it must be okay to bring kids this trip. I'm pretty sure Aunt Rue is coming along too"

"Awesome!" says Micah. "We will have some cool adventures. I hope something exciting happens this time like last time."

"It sounds like you boys are cooking up something over there," Grandma says as she turns and smiles at us shaking her head.

"Oh no, Grandma." I reply. "No schemes here… we're just wondering whether Dad will take us on his next trip."

"I don't want *Magic* to have to fight monsters though." I whisper. "She was almost killed."

Magic jumps up at the mention of her name and wags her tail, seriously looking for a pet or two. "Poor *Magic*," says Jacob as he pets her huge, golden head.

"Your dad sure has a cool job!" exclaims Jacob. "When will we find out if we're going?"

"Hopefully, by tonight." I reply. All I know is that *Magic* will be coming with us too. We never go anywhere without her since last year's trip. She saved the day more than once. She was awesome!"

Magic knows they are talking about her as she starts jumping around and wagging her enormous, golden, feather-like tail.

King Tutankhamen

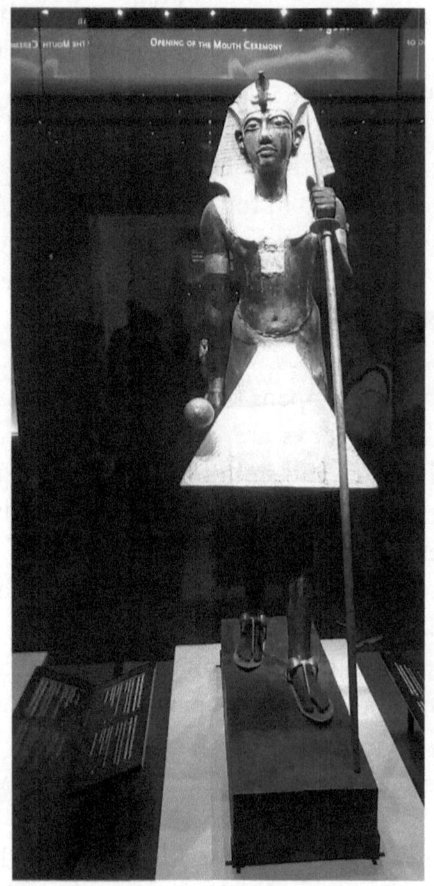

CHAPTER THREE
NIGHT AT THE MUSEUM

"Hey Paul, come quick," says my dad, Noah. "Someone robbed the museum in Egypt. You know the one…where King Tut's tomb is."

"Ruff," barks *Magic* as she rises up from the floor and looks at the T.V. Dad chuckles and pats her on the head.

"You interested in a stolen amulet, *Magic*?" Dad questions her.

I run in to the family room where my dad is watching television. Dad knows I love anything about Egypt and especially King Tut. His full name is King Tutankhamen.

"We just studied about him in school." I reply excitedly.

"I know," says Dad. "That's why this is extra interesting."

The story of King Tut is amazing. He became king when he was eight years old. The historians originally thought that he was killed by a blow on his head when he was in his twenties. After further examination of his body, with all our modern x-ray equipment like cat scans, the experts think he was killed during a battle, which means he was a warrior. The experts believe that he was run over by a chariot because the bones on his right side were all broken and crushed, which would be consistent with a chariot running over him. His tomb was the first undisturbed tomb found by an archaeologist after many years of searching for it. The guy who found it was Howard Carter. He became famous after his discovery, but there have always been rumors of a curse on the tomb. It seems that anyone who has had contact with the tomb in any way has died an untimely death. People think that the tomb should have been left undisturbed, and maybe King Tut, in his afterlife, is taking revenge on anyone who fools with the tomb. Curses and mysteries about discoveries always make them more interesting.

"What's happening?" I ask.

"They are in the process of moving the museum from the Valley of the Kings to Cairo, Egypt." Dad replies. "I guess it is a better location. The security is not up to standard during this move and someone broke in last night and stole one of King Tut's amulets. It is quite the scandal, and someone is going to be in big trouble for letting the robbery happen."

"Which amulet was stolen?" I question excitedly. "There were at least 10 of them, all rumored to have powers of huge proportions."

"Don't tell me you believe that?" Dad teases. "How can an object have powers?"

"Well, it could have a curse on it from a demon," I insist. "Which amulet was it?"

"The news didn't say which amulet was stolen." Dad replies "So… powers you say. What then would the object be capable of?"

"I would imagine it would give the owner power to do evil things." I reply.

"Whatever you say, Paul." Dad chuckles.

"Well, you never know," I reply. "Look at the evil we experienced in Scotland from a dog and a boy last year."

Dad says, "You are so right. I was skeptical then, but I won't be skeptical again about the possibilities of the devil taking advantage wherever he can. I am just glad that this robbery didn't happen in Italy. Egypt is a fair distance away, which is reassuring, just in case some weird stuff starts to happen with the mysterious amulet. I would hate to find ourselves in another terrifying situation. Speaking of Italy, how would you like it if I invited Jacob and Micah to go on our filming expedition?

"Honest?" I question. "Really? You aren't just saying that are you? Would Aunt Rue be going too?"

"Hey, I wouldn't be bringing it up if I didn't mean it." Dad replies. "If Aunt Rue thinks she can handle you three troublemakers in Europe, she is welcome to go. Of course, Adino is also going, so that might influence her decision. I think she has been in contact with him since our trip to Scotland last summer. He must have made an impression on her because she is never interested in any men."

"That will be awesome" I exclaim. "Aunt Rue and *Magic* have to go."

"What's this I hear about me having to go?" Aunt Rue questions as she saunters into the family room." Aunt Rue is short and petite. She has red hair like my dad and me. I guess we all kinda look alike. She is youngest. I am the tallest, and, for that, I am thankful. My dad is short and thin. My dad has a brother who lives in Ireland, but I've never met him. He has blonde hair. I guess the red gene skipped him.

"We're going to Italy," I yell. "Micah and Jacob get to come too."

"What?" replies Aunt Rue. "Are you kidding me? Those two goofballs? Yeah… I know about the trip. Adino told me." Aunt Rue smiles.

"Ohhhhh, now we know." I tease her. "You have something going on with Adino."

"Well," responds Aunt Rue, "if you call occasional emails something going on… well… then I guess you're right."

"I knew you liked him." I say. "Actually, he is pretty cool. I guess I approve. At least he's got an interesting job, kinda like you, Aunt Rue."

Aunt Rue ruffles my hair, "I am glad you approve dude."

"What do you think about Micah and Jacob coming?" Dad asks Aunt Rue. "They can hang with Paul and free you up a bit. That way you can have more time to spend with Adino," Dad teases. Dad and I high five.

"All right you two," says Aunt Rue. "You guys are annoying enough without the other two bone heads. How am I supposed to deal with all of you guys? You will be treading on thin ice, if you think I am going to put up with a lot of stupid behavior or shenanigans like went on during our last trip."

"You'll be off with Adino," I tease.

"Don't be so sure of yourself." Aunt Rue responds. "I don't feel like having another fiasco like we had in Scotland. I find it hard to believe that you three boys will be able to stay out of trouble. That's not even considering the other teenagers you will be hooking up with like last time. I'm not so sure you guys can handle being on your own in Italy without me hanging around to supervise or rescue you.

"So you want to go?" asks Dad.

"Well," Aunt Rue replies, "if they can stay out of trouble, which I doubt, it should prove to be quite the adventure. I hope this time we can avoid fights with monsters and devil dogs."

"Amen to that." Replies Dad. ***Magic*** is up wagging her tail.

Street Scene, Venice, Italy

CHAPTER FOUR
CIAO

Italy, here we come! This has got to be, by far, the coolest thing my dad has ever done. Both Micah and Jacob are joining us on our trip. We have a non-stop flight, which is always great, so I don't have to worry about *Magic* getting lost when we change planes. We will be touring the cities of Rome and Venice in Italy. We will be on this trip for 10 days. Grandma decided not to come this time as she and Phoebe have three weddings to cater, so she didn't think she could leave her business for that long. We will miss her, but last year's trip almost sent her over the edge with all the supernatural and horrifying events that took place. Aunt Rue is always game for adventure, so, naturally she is also joining us. Of course, Adino's presence with the film crew might have some attraction for her. She met him last year in Scotland, and he helped with all the action that went on. He's a cool dude with an awesome Greek accent.

I wonder if the friends I made last year are coming along with their parents. I hope so. They were really fun and ready for everything. We had a blast and became really good friends. Whenever there is trauma, people come together and develop a bond. That happened with my friends and me last year in Scotland. Maybe there will be new kids as well.

"Dad," I yell, "Micah and Jacob are here with their stuff."

"I want to see their passports and paperwork," replies Dad as he exits his bedroom and comes into the hall. "I will be downstairs in a minute. The car will be here to get us in fifteen minutes. You boys better get your stuff by the door and ready to load. Make sure *Magic's* cage is near the door as well. Let her sniff it and go inside it, so she remembers what it is for."

"Okay." I reply as I turn and run down the stairs to greet my friends. Of course, *Magic* is right behind me.

"Hey, you made it." I say to Micha and Jacob. "Dad wants to see your passports and other paperwork when he comes downstairs. Put your bags by the door. Dad says the car will be here in fifteen minutes. I need to get *Magic*'s cage and let her become familiar with it, so she won't be scared when we get to the airport. I have to remember to give her the sleeping pill when we get to the airport."

"Whoa, whoa dude….slow down," says Micah. "You are all amped up."

We all laugh. "Flying makes me nervous." I reply.

"Seriously, dude, it will be fine," laughs Jacob.

"I'm sure glad you guys are going this time." I say. "You know *Magic*, and she knows you. That's really a good thing because she's so different."

"I am not sure 'different' really describes her." replies Micah. "I would say more like unusual. It's probably a good thing we're going along because, if Aunt Rue is meeting this guy there, she will probably be preoccupied." We all chuckle.

"What's so funny?" Dad asks as he comes down the stairs. "You aren't already cooking up mischief are you?"

"Oh, Mr. Wonder," replies Micah, "we are really thankful you have invited us. We will try our best to stay out of trouble."

"That's reassuring," replies my dad to Micah and Jacob. "Paul, are you getting *Magic*'s cage?" Dad calls to me.

"I'm coming dad."

"Let me see your passports and paperwork boys." says Dad. "You have to carry your passports, phone numbers and addresses of the American embassy and maps of the area at all times. I hope you have figured a way to carry those things."

"I have them folded up and put in my passport case, and it fits in my pocket." Micah says.

"Me too." Jacob chimes in.

"Here's *Magic*'s cage." I say as I come back into the entryway dragging the cage. *Magic* starts jumping around. We all pet her and encourage her to go into the cage.

"Did you give Micah and Jacob the special phones they are to carry?" Dad asks me.

"Yeah, and I explained how they work." I reply

"Just remember, "Dad lectures, "If you get into any kind of trouble or jam, call me. It is a walkie-talkie as well. They are expensive phones, which are issued to us by the security company. Take care of them. Don't lose them."

"Oh hey," Aunt Rue says laughing as she comes down the stairs, "it sounds like I missed most of the lecturing we are all subject to before a trip."

"Don't you start." Dad replies to her. "I'm just briefing these boys on the equipment."

Aunt Rue rolls her eyes and flips his baseball cap. "You and Paul get so uptight when we go traveling. Relax. What could happen? It's not like anything ever happens when we go traveling." She says as she laughs.

"Dad, the car's here." I say.

"Let's have a prayer together before we embark on this journey." says Dad. "I think God will need to be on high alert with this group traveling."

I always feel better after dad prays. I know God will be watching over us. He always is.

Dad finishes our prayer, and *Magic* is the first one out the door.

Rome, Italy, Street Scene and Colosseum

Chapter Five
The Getaway

"We did it. It all went as planned." Abel exclaims as they stand in the abandoned warehouse they met in before the theft. "I can't believe it worked, and we've got the amulet."

"You worry too much." says Samson. "We had it in the bag."

"Don't get too cocky, now." warns Abel. "We still have to get out of the country and enter another country. I am glad we decided to hide out in Venice. With all those canals and nooks and crannies, no one will be able to hunt us down, even if they discover who took the amulet."

"No one will ever track the robbery to us." reassures Samson. "They didn't know what hit them. The place was in an uproar with all the moving of everything. I gotta hand it to ya, Abel. You really planned the heist of the century this time. It'll be all over the news"

"Well, let's not get careless." replies Abel. "We aren't home free yet. We'll hide out for a while and then go back to the states, where we can really test the powers of this treasure and check out the possibilities of selling it on the black market."

As they are standing in the abandoned warehouse discussing their next plan of action, the getaway van, holding the amulet, starts to glow and becomes a fiery red. It emits a high pitched sound that the thieves can't hear. They have their backs to the van and are oblivious to the glow of the van.

"Let's get going to the hotel." says Abel. "We've got a flight to catch in the morning. I won't be calm until we get home free to Venice."

They adjourn and head toward the van. The van has stopped glowing, but there is a rancid smell engulfing them. It smells like Sulphur or rotten eggs. They all wince and cover their noses. "What in the world is that smell?" complains Abel.

"Geez. It smells like someone died." Jonah whines. "Let's get in the van and get out of here." He reaches the van first and grabs the handle of the van, and he lets out a blood curdling scream as he falls to the ground.

"What happened?" shouts Abel.

"The...the... handle. Blasted hot!!! Get away from it," shouts Jonah.

They rush over to look at his scalded hand and help him get up.

"What did you do?" screams Samson. "Are you trying to get us caught? Stop screaming!"

"He's hurt, you idiot." shouts Abel. "Let's get out of here before something else happens."

"I'm not getting in that van." cries Jonah. "It attacked me."

"Are you kidding?" Samson questions. "The smell is gone, at least. Someone test the handle to see if it's hot."

"Why don't you test the handle?" whines Thomas.

"Take off your shirt." Samson commands Saul.

"All right, all right," responds Saul. "Calm down." Saul is the spineless, squidly brother of the financier of the project. His brother sent him along to keep an eye on this motley crew.

Saul takes off his shirt and hands it to Samson. Samson wraps it around the handle and opens the door. The stench that they smelled earlier comes wafting out of the van and almost knocks them over. They crouch down covering their faces.

"Geez, what is that smell?" Samson questions.

"We still don't know if it's safe in the van," whines Thomas. "Did the handle feel hot through the shirt?" he questions Samson.

"No. I don't know what happened," Samson says. "Let's go. Quit being a bunch of sissies."

They cautiously pile in the van. Samson starts the engine and backs out of the warehouse.

Rome, Italy, Pantheon

CHAPTER SIX
WHEN IN ROME

"I can't believe we're in Rome!" exclaims Micah. They are standing around waiting for the luggage to come out on the carousel at the airport. "They sure unload the animals quickly."

"Yeah, I am always anxious until I get *Magic*," I reply as I pet her head. She looks at me, tongue wagging and those golden eyes slightly glowing.

"Pretty cool, huh?" I reply. "The flight is pretty annoying, but, once we get where we are going, it is worth it. Wait 'til you see the car. It's usually a cool limo. We get to use it the entire time we're here."

"Hey, 'when in Rome, do as the Romans do'," chuckles Jacob. "You know that expression? Does that mean we can drink wine with every meal and eat pizza as much as we want?"

"Yeah, right," I reply, "I'm sure my dad will go for that. Aunt Rue will probably be watching us like hawks, after last year's fiascos in Scotland. Maybe she will be occupied with Adino."

"We can only hope," says Jacob. "Maybe we can talk with Adino and put some ideas in his head about romantic places to take your Aunt Rue. Then we will be on our own."

"We just have to be well behaved," I say, "at least while we are around the adults, so they think we will be fine on our own."

Micah asks, "Is the itinerary you gave us on the plane the exact stuff we will be doing?"

"Some of the stuff we will be involved with," I reply, "but Dad will let us know when we are free to roam."

"Awesome!" Micah and Jacob exclaim.

Here's the luggage." I say as I head to the carousal to haul our bags off.

The limo pulls up at the passenger loading zone for us to get loaded up. It is like a Hummer limo. I guess, since we brought so many with us this time, we needed a larger vehicle to carry our entire luggage and **Magic.**

We all scramble in and get settled. "Wow, this is amazing!" exclaims Micah.

"I told you we travel in style." I laugh

"Check out the bar." Jacob comments.

Dad says, "Don't get any ideas, boys. Your choices will be limited to sodas."

"But, Dad," I plead, "You know that expression.....'When in Rome....act like the Romans."

"Well, well, well," says Aunt Rue, "Aren't we the clever ones."

"Oh you can act like the Romans all you want," replies Dad, "but stay away from the wine."

"Well," I respond, "Jesus did turn water into wine in the Bible for the wedding festivities."

"Yes," Dad Replies, "but the Bible doesn't reference the children partaking...and...where is the wedding? That's all I need on this trip. I can picture it now." Dad holds his hands up like he's setting the stage. "I get a call from the local police because they have picked you up for underage drinking. That should go over well with the director of my film, especially if I have to leave the set to bail you out. She was patient with me last year with all of your escapades. I don't want to push my luck."

"Don't be so dramatic, Dad." I laugh. "I was just thinking of partaking in a little bit of wine when we are at dinner with you adults."

"You better think again," Dad replies. "And you better keep your thought process on sodas."

"He told you." Aunt Rue chuckles as she ruffles my hair. "Don't go sneaking around on us....you're lucky enough to be on this trip... with your friends, no less. I have another expression for you....Don't bite the hand that feeds you."

"Ha, ha, ha, very funny." I reply. "You think you're so smart."

"Hey, at least I know not to push my luck," chides Aunt Rue.

Jacob and Micah look at each other and roll their eyes.

Magic sits up from her cozy spot between the seats and barks with approval.

Chapter Seven
Prophecy

"We can't take him to the hospital," Abel says as they are driving to the airport. "We got to get out of Egypt, before someone tracks us down. Again, what in the world happened, Jonah?"

"I don't know!" Jonah wails. "I grabbed the handle of the van, and it was red hot! It was weird. It didn't look hot… Jeez, man, I wouldn't have touched it, if I knew it was hot."

"Let's go to the store and buy more bandages to wrap his hand and one of those ice packs," responds Samson. "When we get to Venice, Italy, we will see if it needs further attention. Let's just get outta here before someone spies us. It still smells really bad…like rotten eggs.

"Yeah, let's get going." says Thomas. "I'm getting creeped out."

"Just watch what you touch in the van." says Abel. "I still don't get it. Why was the handle hot?"

"Well, you said the amulet has powers," responds Saul. "Maybe it's out to get us."

"Don't be ridiculous!" says Abel. "With the amulet, we hold the power. We are in charge now. Let's not lose our focus. First let's find a place to get some bandages.

The suitcase holding the amulet starts to glow a fiery red in the hold of the van. No one notices as they are all focused on looking for a store of some kind to get some bandages.

Chapter Eight
All Aboard

"First on the agenda is the 'Meet and Greet,'" Dad says as we are driving to the hotel.

The hotel is downtown Rome so we can walk just about anywhere we want to go. We can even take the train because the train station is only one block away. I am not sure how many platforms there are, but I am guessing there are a lot. If we decide to take the train somewhere, we will have to scope out the platform before we go. I am glad that most people speak English. My Italian is not very good. Dad made me learn a few key phrases before I came. I guess that is a good idea.

"What is a 'Meet and Greet?" asks Jacob.

"That's where the film crew meets up to greet everyone who is involved with the film," says Dad. "It usually is at a really cool restaurant, or like last year, it took place at an amazing castle. This time we are meeting at a hotel. The director must be staying there. She usually arranges the 'Meet and Greets' at the place where she stays.

"Maybe we will meet the other kids that are here." I say excitedly. "Maybe even Adino will be here, Aunt Rue." I tease.

"Don't go nosing into something that is none of your business." responds Aunt Rue.

"Well, we'll see what happens once Adino show up." I reply.

"You two better make your peace before we get into this vacation." Dad warns.

"Oh calm down, Noah," Aunt Rue chides. "We are just havin' some fun."

"I'm just hoping that we avoid supernatural incidents this time," replies Dad. "If we have an incident this trip, we may never be invited again."

"You are so paranoid," laughs Aunt Rue. "I'm sure these boys and *Magic* will be just fine, especially since I won't be letting them out of my sight."

"That's what you think!" I reply. "We'll stay out of trouble. I promise. Are Adam and the twins, Anastasia and Delilah, coming with their mom this trip?"

"You know," replies Dad, "I'm not quite sure who is bringing their children. I guess it will be a surprise. We will find out tonight."

"Adam, Delilah and Anastasia are the director's kids," I tell Micah and Jacob. "They are really cool. Adam is my age and I think the twin girls are older. I forget. Well, if they are here, we will get the details."

"Will there be any other kids that you know?" asks Jacob. "Do the twin girls look alike?

"I'm not sure who will be here," I reply. "No, the twins don't look alike. Anastasia is tall with brown hair and athletic looking. Delilah is short and has blonde hair and is not athletic looking. Adam doesn't look like either one of the twins. He's tall, thin and has brown hair. I just hope Judas won't be here. That would be too weird."

"Everything worked out with him," reminds Dad.

"I know." I reply. "But it still would be weird. Hey look, there's the Coliseum."

"WOW!" exclaims Micah. "It's ancient ruins right in the middle of the modern city!"

"That's Italy," responds Dad, "especially Rome, which is why it is such an awesome place to see. The Colosseum is a symbol of the Italian Capital and one of the world's biggest tourist attractions. It is an elliptical building measuring one hundred eighty meters long and one hundred fifty six meters wide. It has over eighty entrances and can accommodate fifty thousand spectators. They also say that over five hundred thousand people lost their lives and over a million wild animals were killed throughout the duration of the Colosseum as it hosted people vs. beast games."

"How do you know all this, Mr. Wonder?" questions Micah.

"My dad always reads up on everywhere we visit and tells us about it while we're on our trip." I reply.

"It's helpful to know what you are seeing when you are visiting other countries," says Dad, "or you never learn anything. That is unless, of course, you are on a tour, which we are not, so someone has to let you guys know what you're looking at and experiencing."

"Thanks, Mr. Wonder." Jacob replies.

"There were also thirty-six trap doors in the Arena allowing for elaborate special effects." Dad continues with his history lesson. "All Ancient Romans had free entry to the Colosseum for events and were also fed throughout the shows. The festivals as well as games could last up to one hundred days in the Colosseum. Sometimes they would even flood the Colosseum and have miniature ship naval battles inside as a way of entertainment."

"Really? That's some cool information, Noah," marvels Aunt Rue. "I knew we brought you along for some reason."

"Very funny," Dad replies.

"It only took ten years to build starting in seventy AD and was completed in eighty AD using over six thousand Jewish slaves." continued Dad. "The major damage was done by earthquakes. There were also gladiator contests, executions and re-enactments of famous battles done in the Colosseum. There is tons of history about the Colosseum. No wonder it's the most desired tourist destination. You boys are really lucky to be on a trip like this, seeing all that you will see. Wait until you get to Venice. There are no cars, only boats. It is really cool. We will have a couple of hours to spare before we have to get ready for the 'Meet and Greet', so I thought we could walk around Rome and explore some of the ruins and Gelato stands before we have to go. How does that sound?"

"Can *Magic* explore with us?" I ask.

"Of course," Says Dad. "You know we never go anywhere without her."

Magic, who is relaxing in her space between the seats, sits up abruptly, wags her giant, golden tail, while she stares at me with her golden, sparkly eyes.

CHAPTER NINE
STREETS OF ROME

The hotel in Rome is old but cool. There are many stories and windows, but it is plain and a beige color. It looks very European with its molding around the top of the building and fancy entry doors. There is a mini elevator which is very rickety. The rooms are small and plain, but there is a great balcony. We can look out on the streets of Rome and even see the train station. Dad and Aunt Rue have one room and Jacob, Micah, *Magic* and I have another. Ours is a little bigger. There are two full size beds and a balcony. Grandma wasn't kidding when she warned us of the tiny rooms in Europe. Oh well, we won't be in the room much. Dad arranged for this room which explains why it is so basic. I just hope the elevator doesn't give out. The large, iron gate that closes everyone in the elevator seems to be on its last leg. There is no air conditioner anywhere and it is hot and humid. Why aren't there any air conditioners?

Dad gives us maps of Rome when we get in our room while we unpack some of our stuff. The maps are so we can find each other if we get lost, along with our walkie talkie phones. We have the American Embassy's phone number and address in case we get in trouble or there is some kind of terrorist activity, and we need to get somewhere safe. The embassy and places of special interest like The Colosseum, The Vatican, The Trevi Fountain, the train station and other ruins are highlighted on the map. My dad has every detail planned when we travel internationally. I get it. We do want to be safe and have a way out, if we get in some kind of trouble. Being in another country can be tricky. There are so many different laws and customs. Sometimes things happen, and the American Embassy can be a big help. Like, if I lost my passport, I would head directly to the American Embassy, and they would help me.

"Dude!" exclaims Jacob. "Our own room! We're living now…and in Rome!"

"This is too cool!" chimes in Micah.

"I told you it is cool to travel with my dad." I reply. "Wait until we meet the other kids and we get to go off on our own."

"What about your Aunt Rue?" questions Jacob.

"Don't worry about her," I say reassuringly. "She will hook up with Adino."

"You hope," Replies Micah.

"Check out the balcony!" exclaims Jacob. "Look, you can see the Colosseum…isn't that the Colosseum, Paul?"

"Yeah." I reply. "Let's go check it out. We have time before dinner."

"Hold on!" Dad comes walking in. "You guys can't just go off gallivanting around without an adult."

"What?" I question. "You said we could cruise around on our own."

"You can." Dad replies. "I just want to make sure I know where you are going, and we will need to coordinate times. We just got here, and I would like to scope out the place before I let you guys wander around by yourselves. Ruthie and I want to go out and about as well, so let's all go together. We will go where ever you want. But…let's start at the Colosseum. I can't wait to check out all the ruins. What a trip this place is! I'll go get Ruthie. Let's go exploring!"

"Your dad is cool." Micah says.

"Yeah, he is, especially since he let me bring you guys. I was wishing you were with me last year, especially since you know *Magic*."

"Ruff," *Magic* says as she jumps up ready to go.

We get down to the street, and the small brick sidewalks are packed. *Magic* is jumping around sniffing the air and is hyped up with all the action. It smells like a combination of exhaust, coffee and sugar. The train is a block away; the Colosseum is two blocks over with bistros and gelato stands winding through the modern streets infused with the ruins. What a city. The streets are narrow cobblestones with men in suits and women in dresses zipping around on baby motorcycles… maybe mopeds… navigating the harrowing traffic on the two way streets. Taxis are swerving in and out of traffic, barely missing the head on traffic of other taxis, motorcycles and bicycles. *I thought what a nightmare!! I wouldn't want to do anything but walk in this city, and I will be careful even doing that!*

"Oh my gosh!" exclaims Dad. "You boys better be careful while we are roaming around Rome. It looks like one could get into trouble with the traffic alone."

"You ain't kidd'n," I reply looking at my map of the city. "Let's head to the Colosseum. It's down this road according to this map."

"We gotta try this gelato," Micah pleads

"Okay, sounds good," Dad replies. "Pick a stand."

"It's about time," Aunt Rue says. "I have to eat gelato and drink cappuccinos in Rome. When in Rome….."

"Don't you start with that 'When in Rome, do as the Romans do' stuff," comments Dad.

"Oh that's right," Aunt Rue replies. "You don't want the boys drinking wine. I hope you are not going to be supervising me and my wine drinking." Aunt Rue flips my dad's baseball cap.

"Hey, hey, stop messing around." Dad warns.

"Oh, I'm really scared," Aunt Rue chides.

"You guys are worse than us teenagers," I say to Dad and Aunt Rue.

"See, Ruthie, you are setting a bad example for the boys," Dad scolds Aunt Rue.

"Look at all these shops," Jacob comments. "Every other shop is selling gelato. There is even a furrier. I guess it's okay to wear fur here. There are a bunch of souvenir shops. I want to get a sweatshirt... Got to have a sweatshirt from Rome."

"Me too," Micah says.

"Here," I say. "Let's get the gelato here." *Magic* barks. "That settles it. *Magic* has spoken." We stop at a gelato store. It's like a store front. The customer stands on the sidewalk and checks out all the flavors of gelato in the window. A guy stands behind the display and dishes up the order. There are five different flavors: chocolate, strawberry, vanilla, caramel and double chocolate. I am going with the double chocolate.

Everyone but Aunt Rue decides on the chocolate. She gets the strawberry. *Magic* is excited with all the smells and people. Of course everyone is stopping to pet her. Dogs are very popular in Europe. Most restaurants even allow dogs to go in and dine. They are allowed in malls and stores. It's pretty cool, and everyone wants to stop and admire *Magic*.

"This is amazing." Aunt Rue says after sampling her gelato. She gives *Magic* a taste from her spoon. Of course she wants more and begins begging everyone for another taste.

"It tastes like chocolate mousse pudding, only cold and thick like ice cream." I say. Everyone else is silent, enjoying the moment.

"Oh my gosh!" Dad exclaims. "Check out the Colosseum! It looks amazing. Look at the ruins everywhere. It is absolutely incredible how they build this modern city around these ruins. They had the foresight to imagine that people would want to see what ancient times were all about. That is really respectful to the history of their country!"

"Cool, radical, awesome!" we all exclaim together.

"I wonder why they didn't tear all this down to build new." I say. "The whole block across from these modern stores is all ruins. This is really awesome!"

"Jeez," Aunt Rue comments. "How did they know not to tear all this down when they built century after century? In America, we tear all the old down to construct new. We could just as easily build around our old stuff or restore it."

"We better head back." Dad says. "We can come back out and explore tomorrow. We should go get ready for the 'Meet and Greet.' Come on *Magic*…walk with me." Dad took the leash from me.

Of course *Magic* is ready for anything.

Rome, Italy, Ruins

Chapter Ten
All Systems Go

"I can't believe we made it without a hitch." Abel comments as they head out of the airport to get their rent a car. "Too bad we can't stick around in Rome for a while. It looks like a happening place."

"Let's just make our way to Venice and get this amulet under wraps." Samson says. "I want to see what this thing can do."

"Well, it's pretty powerful," Jonah says, "if it can burn my hand."

Samson shoots him a look of concern.

"Get the van, Samson," Abel says. "We'll wait over there by the benches."

Samson looks at Abel with disdain. "What's the matter, your legs broken?" Samson sneers.

"Just do it," Abel snaps.

"Over here, Jonah," Abel says as he heads toward the benches. "Don't pay attention to him. He's just antsy. We all are. Once we get to Venice and can relax, everything will be better. We can probably even take care of your hand. How's it feeling?"

"Horrible!" replies Jonah. "I hope it doesn't get infected. It throbs. How long until we get to Venice?"

"I'm not sure," Abel says. "I think it's about four hours. Maybe we can stop along the way and get you some help. It's not like anyone is looking for a burn victim."

"Four hours," Jonah whines. "Here's the car."

"This is a busy city," comments Samson.

"Well, when we arrive in Venice," Abel says, "we will have to park in a structure and take a water taxi to our hotel."

"How far is it?" asks Samson.

"Four hours," whines Jonah.

"Four hours!" exclaims Samson. "I ain't gonna be drivin' four hours. Someone else can do some of the driving. I'm tired and stressed. I just wanna get there and hide out. You say this Venice place is quiet and remote? Not crowded?"

"Jeez," complains Abel, "what is it about four hours? Stop complaining. Someone else can drive half of the way. Thomas, you can drive when Samson gets tired. I don't wanna listen to complaining… And, yes, I picked Venice because there are a lot of alleys and canals to get lost in, if we need to. No one will notice us. We have a place on the canals. It looks very secluded-away from any crowded areas. We should be fine for a couple of weeks there. All the tourists will be gawking at the canals and gondolas. Besides, everyone wants to go to St. Mark's square, and our hotel is across a canal from St. Mark's Square."

"I don't wanna drive in Italy," Thomas whines. "It looks hectic, and I might crash. Then where would we be? An accident in a foreign country with a stolen amulet that everyone is looking for. Let Jonah drive."

"You idiot!! Jonah's hand is burned," Abel screams. "How do you suggest he drives with a bandaged hand?"

"Shut up, all of you!" Samson yells back. "I will get us out of the city. The country won't be bad to drive through… Just everyone calm down. Maybe, when we pass through some little town, we can get a doctor to look at Jonah's hand. We have got to start acting calmer, if we don't want to attract attention."

"All right, all right." Saul shouts. "I'll drive when we get to the country roads. Are you sure we have to take a boat taxi to our hotel? That sounds complicated."

"Well…your holiness…you are actually volunteering to do something to help?" scolds Samson. I guess if you don't want to take the water taxi, you could swim." His comment draws a chuckle from all of the thieves, except Saul.

"Very funny," Saul snaps back.

"Don't worry. Don't worry." Abel says to Saul. "I have researched the whole thing and know all about travel around Venice. I am the brains of this operation, so don't question the plan. You couldn't find your way out of a paper bag. You're just good at getting into small areas undetected. That's the only reason you are here."

CHAPTER ELEVEN
PARTNERS IN CRIME

"Okay, everyone. Take it easy tonight," reminds Dad as we're driving to the restaurant swerving in and out of the frenzied traffic. "Let's make a good first impression, since we left everyone in such a state after last year's antics. We want to appear that we are calm and ready for a nice relaxing time here in Italy. We don't want even one little hint of trouble. Got it?"

"Good heavens, Noah," replies Aunt Rue, "is it okay to breathe? I will be keeping an eye on these boys better than I did last time. Besides, we are not exploring castles and dungeons this time. What could happen?"

"I hope we are going to be allowed some freedom." I reply as I look at Jacob and Micah with a smirk on my face.

"It's up to you." Aunt Rue says as she eyeballs us boys. "You show me you can be trusted, and we will see what happens."

"I hope some of the kids that came last time are here." I say as I ignore Aunt Rue's warning.

"I'm pretty sure the director's kids are coming." Dad replies. "The thing I am worried about is the atmosphere in Venice. It seems like it might be conducive to mischief. You know....there is a lot of nooks and crannies throughout the canals, and I would hate for anything questionable to be cooked up between all you teenagers."

"Come on Dad." I reply. "What could happen? Someone fall in the water? Explore a quiet street and find a deserted church or something?"

Magic says, "Ruff!" as she wags her tail.

Aunt Rue says laughing, "Oh yeah, you will be in on it too, will ya? Good ole *Magic*. Never misses a beat." Aunt Rue pets *Magic*, who is at her feet wagging her immense tail, tongue hanging out as she pants. She starts to glow, but I don't say anything. I'm the only one who seems to notice her glowing tendencies, although Sarah from last year's trip also noticed ***Magic's*** abilities. *I wonder if Sarah will be here this year. I better not ask because Aunt Rue will jump on me insinuating I like Sarah. No, it is best to keep Sarah and our friendship* and *her knowledge about **Magic** to myself. I did mention it to dad last year about Sarah noticing **Magic's** transformations, but he might have forgotten. It is best not to mention interest in a girl. Everyone will jump to conclusions.*

"We're here." Dad exclaims. "Remember…

"We know," I cut him off, "Be on our best behavior."

We walk into the restaurant attached to the hotel which looks like it is right out of the Roman archives. There are tall, gold pillars along with statues of famous Romans placed around the circumference of the place. The ceilings are painted to resemble a royal blue sky with white, fluffy clouds and a few gold, plump cherubim's floating around. The tables are spaced so as to give each party privacy. There are plants surrounding the tables for a feeling of being outdoors, and the aroma that floats around our heads is hypnotic. ***Magic*** licks my fingers and brings me back to reality. She must smell the amazing Italian spices swirling with the unmistakable scent of Parmesan Reagiano and Asiago cheeses which are invading our nostrils. I couldn't help but think of my grandma and her amazing Italian feasts and wished she was here. She would be in heaven with Rome and all of its awesomeness.

We follow the waiter up a spiral staircase to the second floor. He leads us out to the balcony, and, suddenly, my friends from our trip last year to Scotland are gathering around us excited that we have arrived. The girls hug me, and the boys and I shake hands and pat each other on the shoulder. Everyone hugs and pets ***Magic*** as she jumps around between them. We shared a lot of adventure and emotions last year. The encounters with the devil possessed dog and boy created bonds of friendship and the realization of God's influences in our lives. None of us will ever forget what happened.

It was a very eerie night in Scotland when we were investigating the ruins of the Urquhurt castle on Loch Ness. (Loch is Gaelic for lake) We were exploring and fascinated by the castle and the amazing canopy of stars that night. Suddenly, we heard this blood curdling scream, and

Magic took off running through some bushes toward the lake. We followed and witnessed this huge, black monster coming out of the lake, his neck careening twenty five feet in the air, getting ready to gobble up the devil dog of Judas, Goliath, with its massive alligator like jaw and sharp, pointed teeth. Its teeth looked as long as the dog. *Magic* raced straight toward the monster right as its mouth came down on Goliath. We were all screaming at *Magic* to stop, but she wouldn't. She soared into the air, engorged like I had never seen her, glowing like a golden fireball in her puffed up glory. She grabbed the monster on the underside of his long neck and latched onto it. The monster screamed, and blood gushed from its neck as it let Goliath go. Goliath went flying and lay in a bloody heap near some rocks. The monster flung *Magic* off and slithered back into the water.

Magic shrunk back to size and stopped glowing and managed to crawl over to Goliath as we all stood stunned at what we had witnessed. *Magic* laid on Goliath and Judas, who had fallen and smacked his head, and started to glow as she licked them. She moved off of them and slowly walked down to the water's bloody edge, her huge, golden head hanging and laid down with her head on her paws.

The earth shook and a weird mist came out of Goliath and Judas, and they woke up as if they had been in a deep sleep. It was bizarre and awesome at the same time. All of us kids shared something supernatural and sacred that night. We praised God that all had worked out well and the evil influence had left Judas and Goliath. It was then that we forged a bond that could never be broken.

I know we are all remembering our adventures and encounters with the devil and evil last year as we greet each other. It all came flooding back to me when I saw my friends. I am so glad that most of them are here.

"Everyone, these are my two best friends, Micah and Jacob," I say as I introduce them to the other kids of the film crew. "This is the directors kids, Adam and Anastasia and Delilah…they're twins even though they don't look like it." Everyone chuckles. "This is Jesse from Madagascar and Sarah from England."

They all acknowledge one another and look each other over.

"Hey, didn't Jeremiah come this year?" I ask.

"I guess his dad took another gig." Jesse replies.

"That's too bad." I say. Everyone agrees.

Wow, I thought to myself. Sarah has really grown up. She doesn't look like a little girl any more. Neither do Delilah and Anastasia. This is going to be fun, I thought to myself. Jacob and Micah will be thanking me for introducing them to these awesome girls. We head to our chairs.

"Are we ready for some new adventures?" Jesse says with a glint in his eyes.

"Yeah." I reply. "But we got to keep our ideas to ourselves. My dad is already suspicious about us trying to sneak wine and getting into trouble in Venice."

Everyone laughs. "We have **Magic**." Sarah says. "She's a brilliant companion for us. She can help us stay out of trouble. Remind your dad of that."

Aunt Rue, sitting at the other end of the table, gives me that look of hers that says, 'don't even think of it.' I am glad she's hooking up with Adino. He swooped right in on her the minute we got here. He's cool though. I'm sure we can talk him into letting us have a little freedom.

Of course **Magic** is up and scooting from chair to chair getting all the hugs and pets from all her old friends. A morsel of food here and there is always well accepted by **Magic.**

Chapter Twelve
The Grand Arrival

The thieves pull into the parking garage in Venice near the historic center. There are five structures. Each structure is three stories high.

"We were sure lucky to find a doctor out in the middle of nowhere," Samson comments as he navigates into the parking structure.

"He didn't even question how he got the burn," Abel responds.

"Yeah, well it still hurts like the devil!" whines Jonah.

"Are we gonna have to listen to him whine the whole time?" questions Samson.

"Will you guys stop!" requests Abel. "Let's just move on. We have to hide out here for a few weeks, and none of us want to listen to you two bicker. We have to park the car, get a shuttle transport and catch a vaporetto to our hotel.

"Tell us about the accommodations at the hotel," Samson says.

"We have three rooms for two or three weeks," Abel explains. "We can let them know if we want to stay longer after the second week. The room arrangements are Samson and Saul will room together, Jonah and Thomas will room together, and I will have my own room, since none of this would've been possible without all my planning and preparations."

"Oh yeah," scolds Samson. "You couldn't have done any of this without us or your so called sponsor, so stop patting yourself on the back every minute. No one would want to room with you anyway."

"Come on," Snaps Abel. "We have to buy our tickets for the vaporetto. Geez, it is more crowded than I expected. The hotel clerk said that this was not a busy time because of the heat. She must've been lying. You can't trust anyone."

"Are the crowds going to be a problem?" whimpers Thomas.

"What do you think?" snaps Abel. "Is it easier to get lost in a crowd or when no one is around and all eyes are on you?"

"Check it out," Saul comments. "This is a really cool place. There are tons of water taxis. I could get used to living like this."

"Well maybe we'll leave you here," Samson laughs. "That's more magic for us."

"Fat chance I am gonna let that amulet out of my sight," Saul warns.

"Guys, lighten up…..we've got a taxi to catch. Grab your bags. Here we go," Abel instructs. "We get to go down the 'Grand Canal', something I've always wanted to see. It's a very famous destination. Relax and enjoy. If you take a cruise ship into Venice, you enter from the 'Grand Canal. Saul, I think you gotta good point. This is a pretty cool place. It seems like a perfect place to hide out. Who would ever expect us of anything with all the action from the boats goin on? We're gonna be just fine here. No one will get in our way".

As they hustle down the canal in the boat, the black suitcase holding the amulet starts to glow an amber color as it heats up. It is sitting at the bottom of the hold where the suitcases are stored. No one notices a thing. Everyone is marveling at the 'Grand Canal.'

Venice, Italy, The Grand Canal

Chapter Thirteen
Free at Last

While the adults are meeting with the director in another area of the restaurant during the 'Meet and Greet,' and aunt Rue and Adino are lost in conversation at our table, we kids start planning. We discuss the best parts of Rome and how we should navigate our adventures. We decide to walk the streets and find our way to the famous Spanish Stairs, the Trevi Fountain, and whatever else we find along the way. There are a couple more famous ruins and 'piazzas' (squares with stores and snacks) along the streets that we are sure to run into. Rome is small enough to explore while walking. There are a few attractions like the Vatican in Vatican City, within Rome, that are not within walking distance, but we will have to go with our parents on those quests, if they get any time with us. The Vatican is where the Pope lives. It is supposed to be pretty spectacular, with the paintings and museum and altars throughout the cathedral. Of course, that is what makes Italy so famous and a tourist attraction, the ruins and cathedrals. We have to dress up to go in them. I wonder if *Magic* will be able to go into the Vatican. There is always a line to get into the cathedral, but it is worth it. I'm thinking we would be able to enter without waiting in line as my dad's job always has perks like that. They give the film crew special privileges in other countries because they are filming travel documentaries, which brings tourism to the country.

We all get ready to leave the restaurant, saying our goodbyes. Of course, everyone has to pet *Magic* goodbye and confirm that she will be joining us on our adventures the next day. Everyone is staying in different places this time, so we will have to make a plan on where to meet in the morning. Luckily, we all have the cool phones we have been given by the director of the film. No one wants us getting lost. They sure keep tight reins on us in foreign countries. I wonder if it has anything to do with last year's escapades in Scotland. It seems like everyone is trying to keep a tighter watch on us. Good luck.

"So did you guys plan your activities for tomorrow?" Dad asks us in the limo on the way back to the hotel.

"We decided to meet at the train station." I respond. "We will walk around the streets of Rome and check out as much stuff as we can. We have our maps."

"Ruthie, are you going to accompany these teenagers loose on the streets of Rome?" Dad asks.

"Of course." Aunt Rue answers as she smiles at me.

I'm thinking we won't be able to ditch her because Adino won't be around. But Aunt Rue is cool. She and I have had a lot of adventures that dad hasn't approved of. Since she is a detective, she is always involved in mysteries.

"We will be in staying in Rome for tomorrow only," Dad says, "so get your exploring out of your system because, after tomorrow, we will be heading to Venice, the city on the canals."

Magic barks her approval.

Venice, Italy

Chapter Fourteen
The City on the Water

After a full day touring Rome and the sights, we are looking forward to our next adventure. All went well on the streets of Rome – the Coliseum is awesome. We ate and ate and walked about ten miles. *Magic* was a hit on the cobblestone streets of Rome, especially at the Trevi Fountain located in the Trevi district; the fountain stands eighty-five feet tall and is one hundred and sixty feet wide and dates back to 19 B.C. At the center is a statue of Oceanus, who stands atop a chariot pulled by sea horses and is accompanied by tritons. There are also statues of Abundance and Health. There are natural rock formations and gushing water flowing everywhere to end up in the pool. Its water is from the aqueduct called Acqua Vergine. The fountain is the largest and considered the most beautiful in Rome. What makes it especially cool is the way that it is quiet; we couldn't hear it as we walked along the cobblestone street that led us to it. Trevi means three ways, since the fountain is a converging point of three streets. It is a totally awesome sight. It fills up the entire area where these three streets meet. It is huge. It was, by far, one of the coolest sights we saw in Rome. Of course, the Coliseum is pretty hard to beat. The coolest part about Rome is how these awesome ancient structures show up at the most unexpected times.

We are all anxious to see Venice. It is built on more than one hundred small islands in a lagoon in the Adriatic Sea. It has no roads. The islands are separated by canals. Bridges join the little islands together. There is a Grand Canal thoroughfare. It is lined with Gothic and Renaissance palaces. St. Mark's Basilica is in the central square, Piazza San Marco. It is a famous place where people like to visit, and there are a lot of movies filmed there, which is why we are going to stay in Venice and film such tourist attractions. Sadly, Venice is sinking and tilting. Scientists are always studying the state of Venice because of the rising sea levels. It is still a major tourist attraction. This city on the water attracts visitors because of its architecture and art along with the setting. It was a major financial and maritime power during the middle ages and Renaissance. Symphonic and operatic music also was an important feature of Venice. It was ranked the most beautiful city in the world.

"This is really cool!" I exclaim as we enter Venice.

"I've heard about this place," says Micah, "but could never picture how it would look. It looks like the pictures I've seen, but it is different being here. It feels like a fishing village."

"Yeah, it does." Dad replies.

"Amazing! The water comes right up to the street." says Aunt Rue. "Look at all the water taxis. This place is packed!"

"We have a couple of boats reserved because of all our equipment." says Dad. "We will have to handle our luggage ourselves. We have to get it on the water taxi."

Magic is running around sniffing the water and putting her paws in it. "*Magic,*" I call, "Come here." I'm afraid she will jump in. She loves the water. She comes to me but continues to run back and forth excited with all the action.

"You better get *Magic* on the leash." Dad warns. "I'm sure these people don't want some dog tripping them up."

I get the leash and hook *Magic* up. We are all amused at the scene she is causing.

"Leave it to *Magic* to stir things up." Aunt Rue laughs.

Magic starts sniffing the air and slightly glowing, almost in an alert mode. I am curious as to why she is glowing and acting alerted. I look around expecting to see Judas and Goliath from last year's trip. This is how she acted last year when we were in danger. That's weird. Maybe she is unsure of this strange city.

Magic stops and looks at me. Her eyes have that gold sparkle I see when she is on high alert. I wonder what is here that has her concerned.

We load the luggage onto the water taxi, which are about twenty five feet long with an awning type cover over half of it. When everyone is loaded onto the taxi, we head down the Grand Canal for a special tour before we go to our hotel. The Grand Canal is huge, unlike the smaller canals linking the islands. It's like a sea with all kinds of things happening on either side as we travel down the middle. There are water taxis going in and out of the smaller canals which connect onto the Grand Canal. There are shops, restaurants, churches, piazzas, bell towers and all kinds of people. It is so strange to look at a city with waterways instead of streets. It's cool. There is the smell of food in the air, like we're passing bakeries and Italian restaurants cooking lasagna and spaghetti. I'm getting hungry for some Italian food. My grandma would sure love this place. It has a mellow and relaxing feel. The smell of the canals is strong too. It smells like salt and fish.

"This is really awesome!" exclaims Aunt Rue. "I have always wanted to see the Grand Canal. It's everything I imagined and more. This whole place is covered with water. Instead of streets, there's water. I see how the scientists predict that it's sinking. Look… that must be St. Mark's Basilica and square. Hey Noah, is our hotel near St. Mark's square?"

"I think it is close because we are going to do a lot of filming there." Dad replies. "It is quite the tourist attraction, and there are many scenes in movies filmed there. The Basilica is at the center of the piazza. The producers like to use this particular piazza because it is large with many twisted alleyways, boats and canals to get lost in or to create mystery."

"Listen to you." Aunt Rue laughs. "You sound like you're a true Italian –Irish Italian that is."

"I hate to say it…but…" Dad continues, "when in Rome……"

Everyone groans with that comment. Dad chuckles at us.

"Hey, you guys were the ones who first started the 'When in Rome' comments." Dad retorts. "The only difference is that I am using Italian words while in Italy, and you, underage teenagers, were trying to snag some wine."

"Look… gondolas." points Jacob. "Can we ride on one of those through the canals?"

"Sure." Dad replies smiling at Jacob. "Just stay out of trouble and away from the wine. Speaking of trouble…those thieves that stole the amulet from King Tut's tomb must've got away. Before we left today, the attendant at the hotel in Rome told me that the airports and cruise ships were on high alert for these guys. That is quite the heist. If the authorities do not catch these guys, this will be one of those capers that go unsolved and into the historical accounts and mysteries. Pretty weird. I wonder why they would want to steal an amulet?"

"What's an amulet?" asks Micah.

"It's usually a small carved object made out of gold or jewels that has been buried in a tomb with a royal person who lived in ancient times." I reply. "This particular amulet that was stolen is from King Tut's tomb. Amulets are supposed to have magical powers, which are why they are buried with royalty, so they can be powerful in the afterlife, which was their belief."

"Geez Paul-you and that brain." Jacob laughs. "You always know about that kind of stuff. I should pay more attention in history. I guess I'm more of a math person."

"Maybe it's worth a lot of money on the black market." I respond.

Dad continues to tell us about St. Marks Basilica. "The piazza also has an amazing outdoor restaurant…quite elegant…with an orchestra usually playing for the patrons sitting in the piazza. It's a famous scene filmed in many movies…the square with the many white tablecloths, orchestra playing, pigeons and doves everywhere, surrounded by ancient buildings. It's supposed to be quite beautiful…and very expensive, so we won't be eating there."

"This is gonna be fun!" comments Micah.

"I think we're in for some excitement." Aunt Rue says.

Magic is still slightly glowing yellow and acting very strange as she sniffs the air and paces nervously.

Chapter Fifteen
Monaco and Grand Canal

"Geez, boss. This is pretty snazzy for us." Thomas sneers. "The Monaco and Grand Canal. That's quite a name for a hotel."

"Yeah, well, I spoke with Harod," Abel responds, "and he is so pleased with our performance that he sent us an advance on our reward for doing the dirty work. He wants to make sure we are comfortable and can take our time getting back to the states until everything dies down."

"He didn't have to do anything to reap the benefits of the amulet," Samson whines.

"We couldn't have done this caper without his funding." Abel says. "And would you keep your voice down. He has earned his position in our group. There will be enough magic and money to go around between all of us. This hotel is closer than I thought to Saint Marc's Square. It's a famous landmark. We can explore and relax and enjoy the fruits while we wait for the heat to cool down. We're next to check in. Why don't you guys get out of sight, so we are not a spectacle standing here in this group, especially with Samson's size and his incessant whining."

"Hey, Saul, look at that giant golden retriever coming into the hotel." Says Jonah.

"It looks like he's with that group of kids." Thomas replies.

"They have a lot of luggage." Saul chimes in. "Looks like they are staying for a while. This place is pretty crowded. I hope those kids don't cause any trouble. Hey, that dog is looking at us suspiciously."

"Ha, ha, ha…listen to yourself. Afraid of some teenagers and a big golden dog?" teases Samson.

"I'm not afraid" Saul defends himself. "I just don't want any trouble."

"Well, I for one am glad he's on a leash." Thomas says vehemently. "I wouldn't want to mess with that huge, furry mess!"

"What? I leave you alone for 10 minutes," Abel scolds, "and you are arguing and making a scene already? How many times do I have to tell you to keep a low profile?"

"Oh, calm down." Samson warns. "These ninnies are afraid of the dog with the teenagers. What a brave group you've assembled, Abel."

Samson starts laughing. Abel gives them all the 'evil eye' and says, "Let's go before you cause more of a scene. I've got the keys."

They all follow Abel to find their rooms.

Venice, Italy, Gondolas

Chapter Sixteen
Mystery Hotel

"Be sure to get all your stuff off the boat." Dad says. "With all these people here in Venice, the water taxis are in high demand, so, if you leave something, you may never see it again."

"I like not having cars and roads everywhere." I say to everyone. "It is so much quieter with water everywhere and no horns honking or screeching breaks." There is the sound of water lapping against the boat and the dock, with the quiet hum of the engine. Everyone gets their luggage off the boat and stands on the dock checking out the surroundings. The hotel is about fifteen feet from the dock. There are at least twenty-five gondolas lined up along the water in front of the hotel. It is an old hotel that is four stories high painted white with a red tiled roof. It is very basic looking with windows lined up along each floor facing out on the canal. The name, 'Monaco and Grand Canal' are painted on the front of the building in black letters between the third and fourth floors with the windows between. *I'm thinking that I hope it looks better inside.* **Magic** is slightly glowing as she stands sniffing the salty, pungent air.

"This is it?" Aunt Rue questions as she stands looking at the weather beaten hotel.

"Yep." Dad responds. "This is the name that was given to me. I think it must look better inside because I was told it is a very lavish hotel. Let's go check it out. We are close to Saint Mark's Piazza. Look… across the canal…that domed building. That is St. Mark's Square. This is beautiful. We can eat at the restaurant here on the water and view Saint Mark's Piazza."

"It looks fine to me." Micah says. "I could get used to living on the water. I wonder if you can swim in the canals."

"I am pretty sure you wouldn't want to." Dad responds. "It is supposed to be polluted. Evidently, it used to smell quite badly, so they had to clean it up and find a way to cut down on the pollution, so tourists would still come and visit."

They walk into the hotel and stop in their tracks.

"Geez, you weren't kidding when you said lavish." Aunt Rue teases. "Good grief! Your director sure knows how to live. Is everyone staying here?"

"I'm not sure." Dad responds dumbfounded. The inside is immense. The entire first floor of the hotel is the entrance. There are pillars separating the areas of the first floor. Pink and maroon Italian tile floors cover most of the entrance portion. There is a grand piano in another alcove with ivory granite floors and plants everywhere. It is all decorated in beiges and browns with bright green plush furniture and antiques in one area, while another area has a more modern feel with white leather sofas, contemporary tables and pottery.

After the shock of absorbing the first floor of the hotel, we make our way to the check-in area. "This is really cool." I say.

"Cool doesn't begin to describe this." Jacob responds. "I feel like a movie star."

"Look at this dining room!" Aunt Rue exclaims. "It's emerald green and looks out onto the canal. It is so elegant and appears to be glowing. I love the way they have drapes everywhere with carved and painted ceilings in such colors I could never imagine. The drapery makes everything look so elegant and special. Mom would die to see this! She should've come."

"I think you're right Ruthie." Dad responds.

"I would love to eat in here." I say to everyone as we walk around with our mouths hanging open. We must really look like tourists, but we didn't care. It's not every day you see stuff like this. It's a massive room. "Look at the size of the table and all those candelabras. It must sit fifty people. Maybe we will have dinner here with the crew. You should suggest this place to your director, Dad. It looks like something out of a castle." The chairs are high backed dark wood with scarlet cushions. The ceiling must be twenty-five feet high, with pillars surrounding the room.

Where there aren't pillars, there is gold and beige wallpaper. The gold is velvet. At the base of the candelabras placed on the table is a row of white and orange hibiscus looking flowers that extend the length of the table. There are place settings for at least fifty people. I have never seen anything so fancy.

"Well, I'll do my best to convince her we should all meet here for a meal." Dad laughs.

Magic suddenly attracts my attention as she is standing in alert mode, her body stiff, her tail straight out and her fur is aglow. She looks at me with her sparkling eyes as if to let me know something is up. My attention is no longer on the awesome environment of the hotel but on *Magic* and why she is alerted. I walk toward *Magic,* who is in the doorway and look around the lobby of the hotel, but I don't see anything that might cause her to be in her protective mode. Of course no one else sees *Magic* the way I see her, except Sarah, and she's not here. I wonder where she is staying. As I am scanning the hotel lobby, which is difficult because it is humongous, I see that *Magic* is staring at a group of men across the tile floor. They look like a motley group. There is a giant man, a couple of small weasely looking guys, a nervous, creepy looking kid and an older guy who seems to be in charge. Why would *Magic* be interested in them, I wonder? She does not want to take her eyes off them. One of them spies *Magic* and says something to the other one who looks at *Magic* and our group. Maybe *Magic* senses something she doesn't like about them. I guess we will avoid them.

My dad checks us in and we head to the elevators. The weird group of men that *Magic* didn't like has disappeared. Good. I hope we don't run into them again. This place probably attracts all kinds of people.

We have a suite on the fourth floor. That means we will have a nice view. We crowd into the elevator and head to the fourth floor.

"There's Sarah!" Aunt Rue exclaims.

We all look down the hall and see Sarah and her dad going into a room. She spies us at the same time, and we wave.

"I wonder if Jesse is staying here as well." I say.

"That would be convenient for you and your friends." Aunt Rue says. "There would be less need for all of you to be roaming around aimlessly."

Dad opens the door to the room as I respond to Aunt Rue. "Don't go worrying about what my friends and I are doing. We'll be just fine."

"Oh I am sure of that." Aunt Rue laughs. "Whoa.....I may never leave this suite!" Aunt Rue exclaims as we enter an opulent room overlooking the canals.

It is a large common area. The ceiling is high, about fifteen feet. It is an opened beamed ceiling with dark wood beams. The rest of the room is painted beige with an elegant chandelier hanging from one of the beams in the ceiling. There is dark wood furniture with beige overstuffed chairs. There are hard wood floors, dark like the furniture and the beams in the ceiling. There are three rooms off this main room.

"I can't even imagine what my room will look like!" Aunt Rue exclaims.

"Which one is yours?" I ask.

Aunt Rue looks at my dad and says, "Well, Brother, where will I be staying?"

My dad looks at us boys and asks, "Should we let your aunt pick her room?"

Aunt Rue gasps. "Really? You would let me do that?"

I say, "You get first pick, Aunt Rue."

Micah and Jacob chime in, "Go for it. After all, you have to put up with us this whole trip."

As we are marveling at the rooms and deciding who sleeps where, *Magic* is running around sniffing and inspecting everything back to acting like her normal self.

We walk around and check out all the rooms. Aunt Rue picks the one that looks like a princess should sleep there. It is gold and beige with huge windows draped with light pink satin, hard wood floors done in blonde wood and beige walls and ceiling. The bed has a gold framed headboard with gold satin upholstery. The room is basically gold and sparkly because of all the gold sconces and crystal chandelier over the sitting area. There is a desk and a settee in the sitting area.

We all continue to explore the unbelievable accommodations. We are quiet because we've never experienced such glamor and riches. *Magic* is as taken as the rest of us. She sticks by my side.

My dad picks a more masculine room. It is far less glamorous but amazing still. It is decorated in beiges and dark woods with a sitting area and its own bathroom of marble. It also has massive windows draped with beige satin. There is a free standing sink and a dressing table with lights around it like the movie stars use.

Micah, Jacob and I are sharing a room that is huge. It is more colorful, with sage colored wallpaper, a beige open beamed ceiling, and hard wood floors of tan and white wood. There is a colorful Indian rug and some heavy, beige, satin drapery over more immense windows that overlook the canals. There are three separate beds with beige headboards and beige, fluffy covers. There are black overstuffed chairs and a table. We also have our own bathroom of brown tinted marble and a huge old fashioned clawfoot tub.

It turns out we all have our own bathroom. Of course Micah, Jacob and I have to share one. That's ok. We don't spend much time in there anyway.

"This is the life." Micah says. "Good luck scraping me outta here when it's time to go."

"Jeez," comments Jacob as he throws himself on the fluffy bed, "So this is the way the other half lives."

We all laugh as *Magic* jumps up on the bed and starts dancing around him. She is in agreement.

Chapter Seventeen
When in Venice...

"I will be heading out early in the morning to scope out the areas we will be filming." Dad informs us.

"Is everyone going to be involved?" Aunt Rue asks.

"I'm sure they will break for lunch so you can see Adino." I tease.

"Don't get smart." Aunt Rue responds. "I will thank you to keep your comments to yourself. You haven't heard me saying anything about you and Sarah."

"What?" questions Micah as he laughs and punches me.

"What about Sarah?" I ask embarrassed and defensive.

"Well…she sure doesn't look like a little girl anymore." Aunt Rue answers. "Just saying."

"Keep your nose out of everyone's business." I retort hotly.

"Oh, come on you two." Dad puts his arms around our shoulders. "We're on vacation. We are supposed to have fun, not bicker. I brought Aunt Rue along so she would keep her nose in your business, Paul. After all, last year proved to be pretty terrifying with you kids running around loose amongst castles and lakes with monsters."

"Never mind." I say annoyed. "Nothing will happen this time. Aunt Rue can hang with us all she wants. You can bring Adino too, if you must."

"Oh, well thank you Master Paul." Aunt Rue teases and bows to him.

"Very funny." I respond.

"So what is everyone going to do tomorrow?" Dad questions.

"I want to explore Venice!" Aunt Rue exclaims as she throws her arms in the air in a dramatic gesture. "The place is beaming with nooks and crannies and food and boats."

"We want to explore as well." I respond less dramatically. "Remember, when in Rome, or should I say Venice, do as the Venetians do."

"Yeah, that sounds like trouble." Aunt Rue teases.

Micah, Jacob and I discuss what we should do tomorrow as we are heading back to our room. We want to ride on a gondola, eat pizza and go to Saint Marks Piazza, as it is called.

Magic can accompany us. I don't understand why she was alerted today. Now she is all crashed out on my fluffy bed, eyes glowing softly.

CHAPTER EIGHTEEN
ESCAPE IN VENICE

"Dad must've had to start filming early." I say to everyone at the table eating breakfast. "I hope he got to eat here. This is really cool. I slept so good last night. I think I'm still catching up on the jet lag after losing a day of sleep. It felt like I was sleeping on a cloud. I may never want to leave Venice."

"Amen to that," Micah says.

"I slept really good too," Jacob responds.

"I didn't want to drag myself out of bed," Aunt Rue says. "Did you find the note from Dad?"

"Yeah," I reply. "I wasn't surprised. He was reminding us to be sure and take our phones and maps of Venice with the phone numbers of the American Embassy… in case we get lost..blah, blah, blah."

Aunt Rue chuckles knowingly.

"There sure are a lot of water taxis," Micah says. "This place is pretty crowded. It's nice to be able to sit on the water and eat as we look at the cathedrals across the canal."

"I'm glad everyone likes dogs in Europe." I comment. "It's great the way they give *Magic* water and a treat."

All of us order a different breakfast, so we can share. I get the French toast with sausage, Aunt Rue gets cappuccino and a croissant, and Micah and Jacob get some kind of egg dish, like a quiche. They serve us blueberry and cranberry muffins too. I want to make sure I have room for pizza later, so I pass on the muffins, but they sure look and smell good.

"So where are we off to today? Aunt Rue says. "I want to explore the tiny streets and allies and maybe find a fabulous pizza place on the canal to have lunch. We have to go to Saint Marc's Piazza and the cathedral.

I can't wait to pray in there. Think of all souls that have passed through St. Mark's Basilica and all the prayers that have been secretly uttered in the alcoves. I want to be sure and light a candle and say a prayer for your mom, Paul."

"I want to say a prayer for her too." I respond sadly. *I sure do miss her, I think to myself. Nothing is the same without a mom, even though everyone tries to take her place. That spot can never be filled, except by her.*

"Hey, check it out." Jacob says. "There goes that group of guys that was staring at us in the lobby. They look pretty creepy. Let's let them get a gondola first and head away from us. I don't like the way that big guy looks at us.

"Well don't go sticking your nose into something that's none of your business," warns Aunt Rue. "I don't want to have to bail you out again this year."

"What else you got to do?" I reply teasing Aunt Rue. "Chill out. We'll be fine. We want to have fun too." We all give Aunt Rue a hard time.

"Let's grab a gondola and head over to Saint Marc's Piazza first." suggests Aunt Rue.

"Ok, I'm done." I say. "Is everyone about finished? I want to start exploring."

"Let's go." Aunt Rue says after paying the check.

"Look…there is a vacant gondola," says Aunt Rue. "Grab it!"

"Watch **Magic** when you're getting on the gondola." Aunt Rue says to me.

"Of course." I respond.

We pile into the swaying, colorful gondola and direct the driver across the canal to Saint Marc's Piazza. **Magic** puts her front paws on the edge of the boat and sniffs the salty, moist air as we meander across the wide, wavy canal. The water is pretty rough, but it is really fun as we bounce up and down over the swells. There are ancient buildings everywhere along the wide canal. There is mostly hotels and store fronts. It is really busy with water taxis and other gondolas. This is one of the main canals, so it is very wide. The inner city canals are much narrower and lined with apartments multiple stories high. The tenant's colorful laundry is hanging out the windows on clotheslines. We saw those while we were heading to our hotel yesterday morning. This place is awesome-right out of a history book.

"We're here, and watch that dog" the driver announces gruffly.

We all scramble out of the gondola onto the rickety dock, as the gondola and dock rocks back and forth frantically with all of our large bodies moving around. *Magic* jumps out first. The gondola driver isn't very friendly, especially with *Magic*. I guess he doesn't like to transport dogs, but, after Aunt Rue told him we were part of the film crew, he lightened up. The dock was very unsteady. Aunt Rue grabbed onto my arm, laughing at her instability on the dock.

"Woah," Aunt Rue laughs. "Geez, I feel like I'm eighty years old."

"That's right around the corner." I tease her.

"Sarah, Jesse, Adam and the twins are meeting us at the piazza." I tell Aunt Rue as we walk to St. Mark's square. "Can we take off and do a little exploring on our own?"

"What? Leave me alone?" Aunt Rue replies as we continue toward the piazza.

"Well…you probably won't want to walk around with a bunch of kids," I reply.

"Ah, go ahead," Aunt Rue replies and smiles. "I want to see if I can tour the famous Basilica. Adino is meeting me for lunch anyway."

"Oh, how long were you going to wait to tell us that?" I say teasingly.

"Never mind, "Aunt Rue says, "Just stay out of trouble. Be sure you save time to visit the beautiful Basilica. You guys will be amazed at the spiritual experience of being in such a grand place."

"Most definitely," I say. "Are you going to be okay on your own? Should I be worried?"

"Wow, you really do care about me." Aunt Rue teases . She gives my shoulder a shove and assures me she'll be fine as she is the detective in the family.

"There they are." Micah says as he points toward the massive cathedral.

"Check this place out!" exclaims Aunt Rue as she stops and takes in the scope of the entire piazza and cathedral. "No wonder they film so many movies here and it ranks as one of the top tourist destinations."

We all greet each other, but can't take our eyes off of the St. Mark's Square or Piazza. It is a massive area with lots of people and ancient buildings and a towering clock. Just like dad said…a classy outdoor restaurant, live music, and birds and people feeding them.

"This is pretty amazing," Sarah says and I live in London. "Venice is truly a brilliant place."

"See you later, Aunt Rue," we all say as she takes off toward the cathedral.

"Watch yourselves," she says on deaf ears as she turns even though she is already half way across the piazza.

It is strange to be back together with my friends from last summer. It's like time never passed. It will be fun to have another adventure, this time with Micah and Jacob.

"What are we waiting for?" Jesse says. "Let's get exploring!" *Magic* starts jumping around trying to catch all the pigeons and doves that are scattering in response to her aggressive behavior. Jesse is from Madagascar. He's tall, muscular, dark ebony skin and massive curly, black hair. I think the girls like him. He is a handsome guy, with a great accent. He's the oldest, so we depend on him to keep us on track.

"Can I walk with her?" Sarah asks as she reaches for *Magic's* leash.

"Of course," I say. "She'll like that. I'm sure she remembers you from last year. She never forgets anything. She's the smartest dog. Sometimes it's just scary."

Sarah takes the leash and gives *Magic* a hug. "Remember me?" she says. *Magic* slurps a big ole kiss up her face. Sarah squeals, and we all laugh. "She is a brilliant dog, Paul."

"Where are you guys staying?" I enquire.

"I forget the name of it," replies Adam, but it's down that alley over there." He points across the piazza to a cobblestone road. "It is super fancy with expensive furnishings everywhere. Our rooms are amazing and so are the bathrooms…lots of gold, statues and canape beds with walk in closets, along with a wet bar."

"Jeez," Micah says. "That sounds fancier than ours, and I thought ours was over the top."

"Where to first?" Jacob asks.

"Let's just pick a direction." Adam says. "Look at all the narrow cobblestone allies or streets, whatever they are, that connect up to this piazza. Let's try that one over there and see where it leads us."

"That's fine with me." I say "Let's just make sure we know how to get back. Maybe we should leave breadcrumbs."

"That won't help, cuz the birds will eat them!" replies Jacob.

"Let's go." Anastasia and Delilah chime in. "I want to walk *Magic* too." Delilah says. "I want a turn as well," chimes in Anastasia.

"You're so popular, *Magic.*" I pet her head.

We start winding our way down the narrow, cobblestone allies of Venice. If we call them streets, it would imply that vehicles were traveling on them, but there are no vehicles, only boats. The cobblestone walkways are lined with little shops and restaurants. The shops are tiny, and the owners live upstairs. We pass over little bridges joining one little island to the next. The bridges are short but tall enough for the gondolas to pass under. The interesting thing about the gondolas is that they are all different. My dad was telling me that owning a gondola is quite the profitable and impressive business. It is actually one of the most lucrative professions in Venice. Each gondola is decorated differently. They are all painted black with six coats of paint, but each has unique upholstery, trim and detailing. They are made of two hundred and eighty wooden pieces of varying kinds of wood. The drivers use a long paddle to propel them through the water. It must be hard when the current is heavy.

"Hey look!" I exclaim. "Isn't that those weird guys from the hotel? Over there, lurking around that deserted building….it looks like an abandoned cathedral."

"Stop," Sarah says. "They're looking this way. Pretend we are playing with *Magic*."

We all pretend to play with *Magic* to avoid suspicion. She is not cooperating though. She starts glowing, and her eyes start to sparkle as well. Sarah grabs my arm as we stand watching everyone play with her.

"Do you see her sparkling?" Sarah whispers.

"You see it too?" I whisper back. Sarah nods her head and looks at me with a very inquisitive look.

"Why doesn't anyone else see it?" I ask.

"Maybe she doesn't want them to see who she really is." Sarah responds.

At that moment, I feel a bond with Sarah. She understands *Magic.*

"They're gone," Micah says. "Let's go spy on those creepy blokes." Sarah laughs at Micah's attempt with his British lingo. I could tell Micah is trying to flirt with her. I can see why because Sarah has become very pretty over the past year. Her blonde hair is long and curly, and she has large, expressive, royal blue eyes and small features that go with her petite body. She doesn't wear makeup, I don't think. She dresses very girly too-a dress, sandals and a colorful sweater or jumper as she calls it.

"Do you really want to go spy?" Anastasia replies timidly. Anastasia is the athletic looking twin. She's tall and muscular. She is pretty too, but in a more obvious way. She wears makeup and has short black hair to her shoulders. She has almond shaped, brown eyes and more pronounced features. She dresses in sporty clothes-like wearing Nike nylon sweats, sweatshirt and tennis shoes.

"Why not?" responds Delilah. "We're here for adventure, aren't we?" Delilah, the other twin is pretty but in a more natural way, like Sarah. Delilah doesn't appear to wear makeup but she dresses sporty like Anastasia. They are both into sports… soccer… I think mainly.

"Let's go!" Jacob whispers.

We start walking toward the ancient, stone cathedral looking building where we saw the group of creepy guys disappear. We creep around the building. *Magic* is still on alert, glowing. I feel a little apprehensive, knowing that when *Magic* starts glowing, there may be trouble ahead. Every time she sees this group of men, she perks up and glows slightly.. Maybe they are up to no good, and she can sense it.

"Look… that door is ajar." Adam whispers. "Maybe they went in there."

Quietly, Jesse and I creep up to the door and ease it open. The others wait back with *Magic.* It is a huge cathedral- like place, only it's empty and dark. It smells dank and pungent. We edge our way forward to try to get a better look.

Jesse grabs me, "Look, there they are!" he whispers.

They are standing around in a circle looking at something that appears to be radiating a bright orange glow. Suddenly, the smell over takes us, and Jesse and I gasp and put our hands over our noses. They hear us and turn around to see what it is. The big guy turns and points to us and yells, "Get them!" We dash out and grab the others and run. *Magic* is running with us. We have a big head start because the building is huge. We race down the cobblestone street and duck into another abandoned building and hide behind some pillars.

"Be quiet." I whisper. "They'll never find us here. There are a million of these abandoned cathedrals."

We hear them come into the building. We are all terrified, holding our breath.

"We'll never find them now," one of them says. "They are up to no good, and that dog they have with them is trouble. Let's try and get the dog and threaten them with killing the dog, so they will stop following us."

"Oh yeah, that's a great idea," another one of them says. "Take the dog, and we'll have the whole bunch of them hunting us down."

"We are supposed to be keeping a low profile," another one says. "I think we better lay low for a couple of days to loose these joker kids. They will find something else to do besides follow us."

"They must've seen the amulet!" one of them exclaims. "It was glowing and giving off that hideous smell when they came into the cathedral.

"We'll just have to move it," one of the them says. "There are plenty of abandoned buildings, like this one. We will go get it and move it here or somewhere else. It is a shame we can't keep it with us, but the smell and the heat is intolerable. I hope we will be able to transport it to the states. Anyway, the kids saw nothing…we were standing around a glowing chest…that's all."

"We didn't have trouble getting it from Egypt to here," another one in the group chimes in.

"Did you hear something?" one of them asks as he starts looking around the dark, empty building.

"Let's get outa here. We'll get the amulet," one of the them says. "We've got to move it now."

We stay hidden and motionless until they leave. When they close the door, we creep out from behind a couple of pillars.

"Oh my gosh," I whisper. "Those are the thieves that stole the amulet from King Tut's tomb in Egypt."

"You mean that one your dad was talking about with the magical powers?" Jacob questions.

"Yeah," I whisper. "I can't believe we would run into them here in Venice."

"Well, it's a brilliant place to hide." Sarah says. "There are tons of places to hide. What a bunch of creepy and scary blokes."

"That glowing we saw must've been the amulet." I say. "That smell we couldn't tolerate was probably coming from the amulet too. No wonder *Magic* has been glowing. She could sense there is evil around."

"What are we going to do?" Anastasia whispers.

"Follow them and try to get the amulet from them." I say. "*Magic* can help. Let's catch the thieves."

"Are you out of your mind?" Micah and Jesse say in unison. "We are supposed to be staying out of trouble." Micah says. "We should tell your Aunt Rue or someone to get help."

"No one will believe us." I say.

"Are you sure we should get involved?" Delilah questions.

"I don't want you guys putting yourself in danger if you don't want to." I reply still whispering. "You can help, but I don't want anyone being scared or getting hurt. We'll make a plan. But first let's see if we can find them. They probably went back to the cathedral where we found them. They probably left the amulet there when they chased us. Let's go."

Magic is the first one out the door already glowing. Creeping around the narrow, vacant allies of Venice, we try to find our way back to the cathedral where we saw the thieves and the amulet. Finally, Delilah catches sight of the scrawny guy from the group. "There. Isn't that one of them?" Delilah whispers. "He seems very suspicious and nervous."

"Yeah," I respond. "There he goes…around that building."

As we try to be discreet, we finally catch up to him. He is closing the door behind himself but not before he looks around suspiciously. Luckily, we're hidden under the nearby bridge. He goes in the abandoned cathedral where we originally saw them with the amulet.

"We have to follow them to see where they move it." Jesse whispers. "Over there… we can keep out of view and follow them when they come out. I wonder how they will transport it. Come on…let's go duck in that alcove so we can spy on them."

All of us rush over to the alcove, across from the abandoned cathedral door, to keep out of view. Scrunched together, we wait, scared, afraid to make a noise.

"There…there…they are coming out." Jesse whispers. "Look… they're carrying a chest wrapped in a blanket. That must be how they transport it."

"Here they come." I whisper. "Stand back…lineup behind me."

"I know the perfect place to hide this." The big, muscular guy says as they pass us. "I spied it on the way back over here."

"Quick…one at a time," Jesse whispers. "We can creep up to the next bridge and have a clear view. They won't see us. We can hide under the rail near the bridge.

"Wait…There…in that narrow path before the bridge." Sarah whispers. "They turned down that path. There must be something down there."

"Stay here. I'll go with *Magic*." I whisper. "I'll keep out of sight. *Magic* will remember where they go."

My friends wait anxiously as *Magic* and I scurry toward the pathway following the thieves. *Magic* and I see the thieves turn into an alcove and vanish. We follow carefully and catch up to them. We spy the door they disappear into and notice an alleyway a few feet further from the alcove and door. We hide there, so we can watch to see when the thieves leave. I hear them and duck behind a pillar.

"We have to keep our eyes out for that dog and those teenagers." The one guy says, as they exit the cathedral. "Hopefully, they have found something better to do then follow us around. My guess is that we scared them."

The other thief says, "Yeah, well, if they don't find something else to do, them and that stupid dog will be toast. I will personally see to that."

The thieves walk back down the narrow path and out onto the main walk where they pass over the bridge as the teenagers hide under it on the walkway.

Magic and I duck into the cathedral where the thieves had been. It is really dark, dank and smells like rotten eggs. I know that smell…the amulet must be in here somewhere. We creep around, waiting for our eyes to adjust to the dark. I get out my phone flashlight to light the way. *Magic* disappears behind a little wall and starts to growl fiercely. "Ok, *Magic.* I'm coming." I find her in this little alcove. There she stands, puffed up and glowing. I stop and feel my heart pounding in my chest and throbbing in my head. I hold my breath totally mortified. There stands the chest, glowing bright orange and vibrating. "Geez, let's get outta here before it explodes!"

I gingerly back out of the room, horrified at the possibilities of what we have found. *Magic* soon joins me, looking like her old self. I bend down and pet and hug her sturdy body and soft fur, happy to be away from that thing. "Let's go." I whisper in her fur. I stand and turn to go but can't find the door. It looks different for some reason. *Magic* stands with me and starts to glow again. Oh no, I think to myself. What's happening? A horrible sound like a snarling crazed dog echoes from the alcove filling the whole cathedral. We hear it clawing at the walls and snarling. The walls surrounding the alcove holding the amulet begin to glow and vibrate, while the sound of the mad dog gets louder.

"*Magic,* where's the door? Find it." I demand in a panic. But it is too late. *Magic* has already activated into her fireball protection mode and is launching herself toward the alcove where the amulet is hiding.

"*Magic*, no. Let's go." I scream. In a fiery orange ball, she fills the entrance to the room holding the amulet. She is emitting a high pitched whine that would peel the paint off a wall. I cover my ears. Wow! I start to pray to God frantically and fall to my knees because I could no longer stand. I am terrified that *Magic* will get hurt. The smell gets worse and the sound of the mad dog and high pitched whine is deafening. It seems like an eternity before the smell begins to subside along with the sounds. The room stops vibrating and the glow slowly disappears. *Magic* comes trotting out from behind the wall with a smile on her face, tongue hanging out. She definitely looks pleased with herself. I plop down on my rear from exhaustion and inspect *Magic*. She looks fine. "What a dog." I say as I hug her close to me and pray into her fur thanking God for my angel.

"We have to find the door." I exclaim to *Magic*. I stand up, turn my phone flashlight on, and there directly in front of me is the door. "That is too weird." I whisper to *Magic* as we bolt to the door. I carefully open the door glancing around to make sure we are not being watched or followed. Heading down the path, we pop out onto the main walkway and see our friends.

"Geez! That was a close one." I exclaim. "We found where they hid it. It's in an alcove like area. It's a weird little room. Maybe it used to be like a utility closet. But the devil is in that amulet. We had a close call, but *Magic,* as usual, saved the day."

"Paul, you look awful!" exclaims Sarah. "What happened? We should have gone with you. I'm sorry."

"There is no way I would've wanted you with us." I replied. "It was too scary."

"What happened?" Jesse asks. "The thieves walked passed us, and we were expecting you and *Magic* to be following close behind. We were starting to get worried."

Adam says, "Let's get away from here and get something to eat, and you can tell us what happened. Then we should make a plan."

"We are gonna get killed!" Anastasia says dramatically. "If not from the thieves, the amulet will get us!"

"Nah, nothing can hurt us as long as *Magic* is with us." I reply as I pet *Magic's* head.

Chapter Nineteen
Everyone In?

We eat lunch at this cool little pizza place on the canal. I feel like we are in a movie. The water laps at the concrete below us as the gondolas cruise by with tourists. The air is filled with the aroma of Italian seasonings and moisture from the water swirling around us; the sound of accordions playing songs for the tourists at the restaurant next to ours completes the experience. We all sit quietly lost in our own thoughts soaking up the Venetian experience. ***Magic*** hangs her head over the small railing ensconced on the concrete wall next to us sniffing the air radiating off the water. One thing is for sure, Venice is hot and humid. The temperature is ninety eight degrees with one hundred percent humidity. If it wasn't for the cool stuff we are enjoying, I would be complaining.

"Hey look…there's your Aunt Rue." Jesse exclaims. "I think that Adino guy is with her."

"You're right." I reply. "Should we ruin her time by interrupting her romantic interlude? We could send ***Magic*** over." We all laugh.

"You boys," Sarah scolds. "Let her have some fun. Who knows what is waiting for her if we get mixed up in this amulet scheme. I'm still trying to catch my breath and am scared but anxious at the same time to hear about Paul and ***Magic's*** encounter in that little room."

The mood turns serious. "Yeah…we need to make a plan." Micah says. "Tell us what happened in the cathedral when you found the amulet."

I relay the story as everyone sits speechless. I leave out the part where ***Magic*** transforms because I'm not sure they will understand.

"Geez, Paul." Micah says. "Are we really going to confront this?"

"Is everyone in?" I ask.

"It depends on what your hair brained scheme is." Adam replies.

"Yeah, I don't want to get killed!" Delilah exclaims. "Those thieves looked pretty scary."

"Come on… what could they do to us with *Magic* hanging around?" Anastasia retorts. "You saw what she did to the Loch Ness Monster, and this can't compare to that."

"I hope not." I reply.

"I think we should think about this." Adam says nervously. "We should make a plan because we have no idea what to do with the amulet once we get it. Maybe we should tell the adults."

"Let's eat first and discuss possibilities" I suggest. "Then… I want to go to the basilica and pray. If we ever needed to pray, it would be now. After what *Magic* and I experienced in that abandoned cathedral with the amulet, we definitely will want to pray for as many angels as possible to accompany us on our possible quest."

"Geez, now I am really confident." Adam says smiling.

"Adam's right." says Sarah. "We need to make a plan. I would hate to get caught with the amulet."

"Okay, if everyone is in," I respond, "then let's decide what to do, after we eat."

While we are waiting for the pizza and discussing our plan, we snack from a condiment tray with olives - three different kinds - and French bread. The food comes, and we all dig in. It is authentic pizza. It is different than the pizza we have in Los Angeles. It has very creamy cheese and tomatoes and Italian spices with a crunchy crust. The waiter brings lasagna, about five inches tall, cheese dripping down the sides. The lasagna is even better than my grandma's. It has amazing flavor of Italian sausage and several different cheeses. We will be stuffed after this meal. *I'm thinking that we better wait until tomorrow before we try to get the amulet. I don't think I will be able to run after this meal.*

We finish our meal and say hello to Aunt Rue. She introduces Adino to everyone who doesn't know him, and we get on our way back to the Basilica to see the cathedral and pray.

"Do you remember which way to go?" I ask everyone.

"I think it's this way." Micah says as he motions towards a bridge crossing the canal.

"You're right," Jesse says, "because I remember that little Bistro over there. When we were looking for the pizza place, I spotted that place because of the iron tables and potted red flowers, but it wasn't over the water, so I didn't suggest it."

"Yes, you're right." Sarah chimes in. "Let's go that way. It really is a maze here. I can see how one could get lost."

"Yeah, so don't lose us," Delilah laughs as she links her arm in Jesse's. "We all need to stay together, especially with those creepy guys lurking around."

As we walk, we pass tiny shops of all kinds. There are bead shops where the women make jewelry while the customer watches, there are lots of shops with Mardi gras masks. Evidently masks are a big thing in Venice. There are gelato stands and bakery shops. The aroma in the air is delicious. We just ate, and I am ready for gelato. This is a very interesting city. There are clothing stores, leather shops, eateries and old cathedrals, mostly abandoned.

"Up there….I think that is Saint Mark's square where the Basilica is." I say to the others. "Here we are."

The Basilica or church is massive. It looks very gothic with pointed arches, stone and glass. It must be two hundred and fifty feet long and just as wide and probably one hundred and forty or fifty feet tall. There are five domes, which probably have mosaics or painting on them inside as cathedrals usually do. The outside is mostly made of marble. It is beautiful.

"This place is huge." Adam comments. "Let's go in."

Anastasia says, "There's a line over there to buy tickets for a tour. Do you guys want to take a tour?"

Jacob responds, "Well… how much is it?"

"I don't know." I reply

"Look, over there." says Micah. That looks like a sign with the prices."

"Can't we just go in by ourselves and explore?" Jesse asks.

"I'm fine with that." I reply. "I just want to go in and see the inside and pray."

Everyone agrees. There is a slight problem. *Magic.* We all stop as if we thought about it at the same time.

"Well, you finally made it I see," says Aunt Rue as her and Adino walk up holding hands.

We all look at each other and smirk.

"Hey, you're just in time Aunt Rue." I say. "We want to go into the cathedral, but I am thinking they probably won't be too happy if **Magic** is with us. How about you and Adino dog sit?"

By this time **Magic** has already run to Aunt Rue and Adino and is hopping around begging for hugs and pets.

"So have you two been having fun?" I tease Aunt Rue.

"Never mind what I've been doing." Aunt Rue replies. "What have you guys been up to? I hope you don't have any schemes planned."

We all stand there a little too quiet which could be suspicious, so I reply as upbeat as I can. "Oh, we just ate pizza and lasagna at that little café on the canal where we saw you, and then headed to this cathedral. So here we are."

"Likely story," Aunt Rue replies with a smirk on her face.

"What?" I reply, while everyone stands around awkwardly. Luckily, **Magic** starts tugging on the lease to go chase the birds.

"Off we go." I hurriedly continue as I hand **Magic** over to her. "Where will you be when we come out?"

"How long are you going to be in there?" Aunt Rue probes. "Are you taking the tour? And I don't remember saying I would dog sit."

"No, we don't need the tour." I reply. The others start walking toward the cathedral. "We should only be in there for about an hour. Please...you know you want to spend some quality time with **Magic.**"

"Okay." Aunt Rue responds. "You better hurry up and catch your friends. We'll be around here in an hour. It is amazing in there. Enjoy and take your time."

"Thanks." I reply as I run to catch up with the gang. We all enter the cathedral and look at each other.

"That was a close one." Sarah says. "I wonder why she is suspicious of us. Are we that obvious?"

Micah says, "Paul, Jacob and I have a reputation of stumbling upon problem situations and then getting involved in solving them, and then there was last summer, of course, when you and Paul got tangled up with the Loch Ness Monster."

"Oh, I see," Sarah says. "Junior detectives." Everyone finds this humorous and we continue into the amazing cathedral.

"This place is incredible." Jesse exclaims as we all stand around with our mouths agape looking at the ginormous expanse of the cathedral, the mosaics and gold. "No wonder this place is known as the 'Church of Gold.'

Everyone starts wandering off on their own to explore and take advantage of this sacred place. I can surely feel the presence of God in this place where so many people have come for hundreds of years to pray. This is definitely hallowed ground. I almost feel like I should kneel to pay my respects.

This church is the most famous of the city's churches. It is the best known example of Italo-Byzantine architecture. It has been the city's cathedral since 1807 and was a symbol of Venetian wealth and power from the eleventh century. It was originally dedicated in 1084. I feel like I could get lost in here for hours exploring the private chapel areas, sculptures, mosaics and gold… lots of gold.

Venice, Italy - Saint Mark's Square

Chapter Twenty
Saint Mark's Basilica

"I don't mean to sound cheesy," says Adam, "but what a spiritual experience! Can you imagine all the prayers that have been prayed in this cathedral?"

"Blimey." Sarah responds. "The little alcove chapels are brilliant."

"If we ever wanted a prayer answered," I reply, "this is the place to pray. I hope my dad gets a chance to come here."

Delilah and Anastasia come strolling out of the cathedral with Jesse right behind them. "That was awesome." Anastasia exclaims.

"Yeah." Jesse says. "It was pretty awesome."

We all stand around looking at the cathedral and all the other sights surrounding us. There are about 50 tables on one side of the piazza covered with white linen tablecloths. Behind the tables is an orchestra playing some Italian music while the people sit at the elegant tables drinking and dining. Doves and pigeons are wandering around the middle of the piazza pecking the ground for bits the people throw to them. It is an amazing place, this piazza and cathedral. On the opposite side of the piazza are stores and cobblestone alleyways leading in all directions, as we discovered. I see why people travel from all over the world to experience this special Saint Mark's Square. After exploring the canals and cathedral, this whole experience hits me while standing in the midst of this extravaganza. This morning was overwhelming, and I was unfocused, but, now, I feel the magic of this place.

"Where's your aunt?" Sarah asks.

"She said that she would be waiting around here in an hour." I respond.

"Look!" exclaims Jacob. "Isn't that Adino and her at that table. But...where's *Magic*?"

We head toward the table where Aunt Rue and Adino are sitting. "There she is." I say as I spy *Magic.* She is lying on the ground on the other side of the table.

"Hey!" Aunt Rue says. "Wasn't that amazing? It is so beautiful! I'm glad you spent some time in there. I hope you prayed for a drama free vacation." Aunt Rue and Adino laugh.

"Yeah, yeah." I reply. "Stop worrying about us. How was *Magic*?"

"She loves harassing the birds. I had to coax her over here behind the table, so the birds were out of her sight. Other than that, she's been good." Aunt Rue replies.

"Thanks for watching her." I say. "Come on *Magic*, let's go." I grab her leash as she jumps up and greets all of us.

"Where are you off to now?" Aunt Rue asks.

"Oh we're just going to do some more exploring." I reply.

"Your dad wants us to meet for dinner around seven. Just catch the gondola back around six, so you have time to clean up. Stay out of trouble." Aunt Rue says as we take off across the piazza.

"Okay." I reply.

"Now what shall we do?" Delilah questions with enthusiasm as we head down an alleyway off the piazza on the opposite side from where Aunt Rue is sitting. "I thought we were going to make a plan to rescue the amulet."

"Well, well." says Jesse. "It sounds like someone has had a change of heart. I am all for this little adventure as well."

"Yeah, wait 'til things get scary, and she'll be the first one running!" Anastasia chides her sister.

"As if you are Nancy Drew," Adam teases his sister.

"After what happened in that cathedral when *Magic* and I found the amulet, I'm surprised you want to pursue this at all." I say. "Let's find a place to sit down. We should be heading back to the hotel pretty soon. It's five fifteen. I don't know how long it takes to hail a gondola. Does everyone have cash? I think it cost forty dollars this morning. My dad will pay us back. I just don't want to be late for dinner. It might arouse suspicion."

Adam says, "There… let's sit at those tables and discuss this caper of ours," as he points to a group of metal tables with red and white checked tablecloths situated along the canal,

We sit down and discuss all the possibilities of recovering the amulet while, again, the smell of Venice is overpowering with the sweet smell of pastries and gelato and the awesome smell of spices. The place is packed with tourists and locals. It's an amazing place to visit and experience this city on the water.

Everyone seems eager for adventure. It is going to be tricky, even with **Magic**. "Let's do it tomorrow morning, early, before they move it." Micah says. "How are we going to touch it?"

"Let's leave that to **Magic.**" I say.

"Are you kidding?" Adam says. "She might get hurt."

"Not **Magic.** She is a special dog. I don't know why or how, but she does amazing things." Jesse says.

At the sound of her name, **Magic** jumps up and starts dancing around. She is ready for action.

Chapter Twenty-One
A Wrench in the Works

"Okay…smarty pants. What now?" Samson questions Abel as they all sit in Abel's suite.

"They're a bunch of kids," Abel replies. "They have probably already moved on to more exciting things now that they have discovered deserted cathedrals. You know teenage boys. They have one thing on their minds….girls."

"But that dog," whines Thomas. "He or she is scary!"

"A bullet to the head will solve that problem." Samson replies laughing.

"Oh yeah….that's great thinking." Abel sneers. "Let's just draw attention to ourselves."

"What I don't understand," Jonah says, "is why those kids even noticed us, and, even more, why did they follow us to see what we were up to?"

"They have no idea what we're up to," snaps Abel. "How could they possibly know anything about what we are doing? They are looking for adventure and sex in Venice….trust me. Those boys have more on their mind then tracking us. They probably wanted to have an adventure."

"I don't care what you say or think, Abel." Samson interjects. "Those kids and that dog are trouble. We need to move that amulet every day just to keep it safe. Maybe we should go back to the states sooner then planned or head somewhere else. We all have our weapons, and I think I'll take some rope and a few tranquilizers, just in case we come across those jokers when we move the amulet. Trust me. I will shoot that dog first if I have to."

"Oh, come on guys!" exclaims Abel. "Let's not make this more dangerous than it is. If we encounter the teenagers and the dog, we'll take whoever is available to use for leverage, or, better yet, talk our way out of the situation. Saul is a smooth talker. I am sure with a little creativity we could avert their attention away from whatever they think they have on us. Above all, let's keep calm and even befriend them. They are a bunch of dumb teenagers. We could befriend them, if we run into them again, and bribe them with booze. What teenage boy doesn't want to try drinking on a vacation in Italy."

"Yeah…" Saul says. "The parents will trade anything for kids. Let the dog be. It's not going to be our 'Ace in the Hole.'

Samson responds, "I'll shoot them all if I have to. We need to make a plan to get out of here ASAP. Let's move the amulet a couple more times and head back to the states. I think things have cooled down enough for us to head out. Call the boss, and see what he says."

"I don't want to drag him into this," replies Abel. "He'll think we're incompetent."

"Just tell him we've hit a snag," says Samson, "and that this place is teaming with officials because of the filming crew that's here shooting a film.

"Let's just move the amulet today, and see what happens," pleads Abel. "I think all will be fine. Those kids have moved on…but…if we encounter anything, we need to have a plan."

All the thieves agree, and they hatch a plan.

Chapter Twenty-Two
The Venetian Amulet

All systems go. We kids have a plan. I hope everyone keeps their cool, so we can get the amulet and take it to the police. It was hard having dinner with dad last night, trying to be calm and interested in his conversation. I guess he's going to fit St. Mark's cathedral into his schedule today. I hope nothing happens to prevent that, like us getting killed trying to grab the amulet.

My friends and I are supposed to meet at Saint Mark's Basilica at 8:00 a.m. sharp. I hope the gondolas are running, and I hope Aunt Rue isn't nosey. Once we meet, we will be off to rescue the amulet. We are all going to creep into the abandoned cathedral where the amulet is, hopefully. *Magic* and I are going to continue a little ahead of everyone while we make our way to the little room where we had seen the chest housing the amulet. I'm going to throw open the chest, and *Magic*, I hope, will know to grab the amulet. The others are going to be at the opening to the room calling *Magic* and coaxing her to bring it to them. I am thinking that *Magic* won't be hurt by it. She's never been hurt. I witnessed the fights in Scotland where she was bloody, and the blood and wounds disappeared. Sarah is bringing a sturdy, leather handbag to put the amulet in, as we probably won't be able to touch it, from what I've seen of it and its power. The twins are going to be on the look-out at the entrance of the abandoned cathedral. If they see anyone coming, they are supposed to run to us, and we can all hide as it's really dark in the cathedral, and there are a lot of pillars. Hopefully, it all works out. It seems like a good plan.

"Hi, Sarah," I say as I meet her on the elevator. "Are you nervous?"

"A bit," Sarah responds. "It's not every day I'm involved in rescuing a magical amulet from a bunch of dodgy thieves." I grin at her as we get to the lobby.

"Where are Micah and Jacob?" Sarah asks.

"They are running a little late and said they'd meet us in the lobby." I reply. "I think they are a little nervous too but won't admit it. Did you bring the leather handbag?"

"Yes, got it." She says as she pulls out the small leather bag from her larger shopping bag.

"Let's sit over on those cushy sofas," I suggest.

"I have a feeling Aunt Rue might be a little suspicious when she wakes up and finds us gone." I say.

"Do you have something planned out to tell her?" Sarah asks.

"Yeah... I am going to say we wanted an early start because of the heat." I reply

"That's exactly what I told my dad last night when he asked about my plans today!" Sarah exclaims. *Magic* yelps and we exchange glances. It seems *Magic* always knows our plans and what we're saying.

"Here they come." I say as I spy Jacob and Micah. "It's about time." I say as I shove Micah.

"Jacob is really slow." Micah says. "His hair has to be perfect." We are amused as Jacob grabs Micah around the neck and starts to take him down.

Sarah and I ignore them, but a hotel attendant walks by and raises his eyebrows. I guess we shouldn't be rough housing in this fancy hotel.

"Knock it off, you guys." I say. "That guy just gave you the 'eye.'"

"He started it," Micah whines.

"Come on, let's go." I say. The hotel is deserted except for the workers getting things ready for the day. "Let's try and grab a scone or croissant at that coffee place. I need to have something on my stomach if I am going to re-steal an amulet."

"Shhhh," Sarah scolds. "Do you want someone to hear?" Micah, Jacob and I tell her to chill out because it's going to be a piece of cake. *Magic* trots along eagerly like she knows we are on an adventure. I suddenly start to get a little uneasy about *Magic* possibly getting hurt. I silently pray asking God to send many angels to us today to help *Magic* and keep us safe. I prayed last night about our whole escapade knowing that God would be protecting us through *Magic*. I know he sent her to watch and take care of me. I just pray it all goes as planned.

"I hope you're right," Sarah says as we walk through the hotel. "I would hate this to be my last day on earth."

"*Magic* and I will not let anything happen to you or Anastasia or Delilah." I reply as I stop and look at her reassuringly. "I promise."

"I trust you," says Sarah as she grabs my arm. "I'm just kinda a chicken."

"I think we all are." Micah says.

We grab a bag of scones and head outside.

Luckily the gondolas are already running the channel, so we hail one and hop aboard.

"Watch the dog!" the driver says.

"She's fine." I reply wondering what is with these gondola drivers and dogs. There must be a lot of dogs that ride these gondolas. It seems like we see a lot of dogs around. Maybe people don't mind their dogs, and they intimidate the drivers.

The water is super choppy and we are getting splashed as we cross the canal. *Magic* sniffs the air and enjoys the water droplets. It does feel cool because it is already hot and muggy this morning. There are already many gondolas rushing about, stirring up the water as well. *What a cool place to have an adventure, I thought. Actually, Scotland was a pretty cool place to have an adventure as well....all those haunted castles we explored.*

"There they are." I point across the piazza as we disembark the gondola.

"Hey!" Adam yells as he waves at us. *Magic* bounds over to greet our friends.

The twins look a little serious. Jesse is kidding around trying to cheer them up. I think we are all a little nervous. Everyone gets cheered up seeing *Magic* with her smiling face and her giant feather- like tail seriously wagging.

"Are... you... sure we need to do this?" Anastasia asks as she pets *Magic.*

"Yeah, honestly… do we really care if the amulet is recovered?" Delilah asks.

"If you girls…or anyone doesn't want to participate, please don't feel you have to." I say to everyone. "It's not like we have to do this. I guess we could tell my dad and Aunt Rue. I think they won't believe us. Maybe they could help. But seriously, with *Magic* beside us, nothing will harm us."

"Okay everyone." Jesse says. "What could happen? Let's think of the scenarios. We could get there, and the amulet could be missing, or we could get there and run into the thieves, at which time, we would run and hide, and *Magic* would scare them. If either one of those possibilities happens, we won't try again… Deal?"

"Yeah…okay. That sounds like a plan." I respond. Everyone agrees. *Magic* yelps and smiles as we all high five.

"Let's review our plan." I suggest as we walk off to the side of the piazza near a cobblestone alley.

We review everyone's role and head to the abandoned cathedral. At least we know where the cathedral is this time. Jesse is right. What could happen? We make our way through the alleyways of Venice, *Magic* sniffing every nook and cranny. There aren't many people out, and none of the shops are open. It is different how businesses are run here in Italy and most European countries. Most stores and restaurants open about ten o'clock in the morning and close at one o'clock in the afternoon. That is when everyone eats a late lunch and rests. Then everything that closed opens again at four o'clock in the afternoon and stays open really late. People eat dinner at around nine o'clock at night. It is a different lifestyle. It is much more relaxed.

"There's the alley." Adam says. We all stop and look around. Everything is pretty deserted.

Maybe it would be better if there were people meandering around, I think.

"Do you think we should wait awhile?" I suggest. "You know… with more people walking around, we might be less conspicuous, and, if we do get caught, the thieves couldn't do anything with everyone out and about."

"I think it's now or never." Jesse says. "It's down the alley, so no one will notice."

"I agree," says Adam. "We can't let our plan go to waste. We have spent a lot of time planning this. It will be exciting."

"Yeah…he's right. Let's just do this mischief." Sarah says as she giggles nervously.

"Okay…let's go." We all say.

"You girls hang around the entrance and keep your eyes peeled." I instruct Delilah and Anastasia. "If you suspect anything…anything at all…come get us. Don't worry about jumping to conclusions…just get us if you are scared."

"We will." Delilah and Anastasia respond.

"Okay… here we are," I whisper as we approach the door.

"Should we hang around outside the door?" Delilah whispers as the others go inside.

"I think maybe you should hang around just inside the door so you can't be seen, but you can peek out and keep watch." Adam suggests. "That way, if you spy something suspicious, you can run to us quickly."

"Okay." Delilah and Anastasia whisper as they hug everyone nervously.

"Watch where we go," I instruct the girls. "Use the flashlight on your phone. It's a really bright light. You will need to know where to get us if you suspect anything."

"Come on…let's go." I say.

We all enter the cathedral. "Shhhh…" I whisper. "We don't want it to hear us."

"If it's still here," Adam whispers.

"Get behind me." I whisper. "Let *Magic* and me go ahead. Keep us in your sight though. Use your lights on your phones. Remember, stand at the doorway and call *Magic* after she snatches the amulet. Then get out the door and run like crazy. I'll be right behind you. Don't worry about me…just run!"

We creep silently through the dark, musty smelling cathedral hoping our eyes adjust to the dark soon. Adam flips on his phone light. *Magic* creeps along as well, as if she knows we are on a mission. We finally get to the little room at the back of the building. I stop and turn to face the others.

"This is it… The chest is still here" I whisper, voice trembling. "Wait here. Get the bag ready."

I grab *Magic* by the collar for reassurance. We edge our way to the chest… so far, so good. There doesn't seem to be a reaction from the amulet yet. I start to smell something rancid. *Oh know, I think.* I pray quickly-"Please God, let this work."

We get to the rather small, black leather trunk. I didn't notice the details of the trunk the first time we saw it…everything had been too wild and surprising. There is a lock on it. It smells really bad. It is starting to glow, and *Magic* puts her nose on it. Suddenly, the smell disappears, and the trunk stops glowing. "Good dog!" I whisper. "The lock," I whisper in **Magic's** fur by her ear. She puts her mouth on the lock, and it falls off the trunk. I flip the top open and there sits a sparkling gold amulet about four inches long and four inches wide. It is in the shape of a bird with an Egyptian head with wings and a curled serpent tail.

"GRAB IT," I say to *Magic.* She grabs it, but not before I hear the twins scream with the sounds of men's voices and scuffling coming closer. We both stand frozen. *Magic* starts to glow and puff up.

"Run!" Jesse screams.

"Get them." A man's deep, booming voice echoes in the cathedral. "Over there…they ran over there."

"Paul!" Sarah screams. "Get ou…." But her voice is muffled.

"Shut up, girlie!" another guy's gravelly voice echoes.

The big dude comes toward *Magic* and me…but he's too late. *Magic* puffs up in all her glory, glowing like a fire ball and charges toward the guy. He doesn't know what hit him. She soars over the others like a rotating fire flurryl knocking down the other two thieves in her path.

"Go *Magic*….Go…" I scream frantically. "Get help!" In an instant she's gone blazing out of the cathedral with the amulet.

The big dude recovers and grabs my foot as I'm running out of the little room to follow *Magic.* "You aren't going nowhere, you scrawny red-headed, snot-nosed kid." He screams as he pulls me along the hard, cold floor. "Get the dog!"

I hear scuffling and yelling. "You'll be sorry you messed with us!" Micah yells.

"You have no idea what's in store for you once **Magic** comes back." Jacob yells.

"Shut up….gag them…Abel." One of the thieves instructs.

I try to struggle with the big dude that has my leg, but he is massive. He twists my leg like he's going to snap it off.

"Okay….okay…" I say. "Take it easy. I'll stop struggling."

"I told you these kids and their dog was up to no good!" The big dude says to the other guy, Abel, who's short, skinny and bald but seems to be in charge, as they get all us kids rounded up at gunpoint. "Did you see that dog leap or FLY over all of us? What kind of dog is that? What was that?"

"I don't know," replies Abel sharply. "Maybe it's a flying dog. Is the amulet still in the trunk? Jonah, get the trunk."

"Me?" The scrawny thief, Jonah, with the bandaged hand whines. "I don't want to get hurt again."

"Take the gun, Jonah," The bald guy, Abel, says as he hands Jonah the gun as he shoves Sarah and the twins against the wall.

"Hey, you better watch that." I yell at the guy, Jonah, who's shoving the girls around. By now I was standing with Jesse, Adam, Micah and Jacob with three guns pointing at us.

"Or what?" the big dude laughs. "I'm really afraid of a scrawny, wimpy teenager."

"The amulet is gone, Samson!" Abel exclaims to the big dude, who's obviously Samson, as he turns from the little trunk.

"This one probably has it." says Samson. "He was the one by the trunk when I caught him."

"So…where is it?" Abel shoves me against the wall his hand around my neck pinning me against the wall.

"He doesn't have it!" Sarah screams. Abel lets me go. *For a puny guy, he sure is strong, I think to myself,* as I cough and spit and rub my neck. I slump to the floor.

One of the thieves holding his gun on us, who has been quiet up till now, shoves his gun at Sarah. "Shut up. One more scream out of any of you… and you will be toast." This guy is tall and gangly, with a red baseball cap pulled down on his face and is wearing a heavy army jacket.

Micah says, "Oh yeah…like a gunshot won't bring everyone running! Please…how stupid do you think we are?"

Samson starts laughing as he pulls out a pipe like thing and puts it over the tip of his gun. "I'd say you're pretty stupid screwing around with the likes of us and thinking you could steal this amulet and get away with it. Now… who has the amulet?"

"That won't muffle the sound enough in this echo chamber." Laughs Jesse trying to show the men we aren't scared.

Abel and the quiet, tall, gangly thief, with the baseball cap, bend down to the bottom of their pants and each pull out thick, curved bladed knives about 10 inches long and brandish them in front of us. "These won't make any noise!" taunts the quiet gangly one. All the thieves start laughing.

"Except for this one here," Samson points to me, "catching these kids was a piece of cake. I told you they followed us and would come back to snoop around."

"Search that kid. He must have the amulet," one of thieves says, who's wearing sunglasses and a black and white bandana wrapped around his head. He has a scar down the side of his face and looks incredibly mean. He's small too.

The big guy, Samson, starts roughing me up. "I don't have it. Get your filthy hands off me." I say.

"Oh…well…aren't you a tough guy." He laughs.

"The dog took it." Adam yells.

"I told you to keep your voices down," the thief with the baseball cap says as he holds the knife to Adams throat.

"Don't hurt him!" Anastasia cries. Both of the twins start crying and clinging to each other.

"Oh ain't that sweet…what a group of pansies you guys are," Jonah, the timid guy with the bandaged hand, says.

"Where is the amulet?" the guy, Abel, who tried to strangle me, says. We all stand mute. "Okay then," he says as he grabs Sarah and starts to haul her away. "This is a pretty little one, nice and petite. She shouldn't be a problem, will you sweetheart?"

I yell, "The dog has it." Abel stops, turns and looks at me as he continues to drag Sarah away into the shadows.

"The dog?" The thieves all start laughing. "Yeah…right," he says as he continues to drag Sarah while she kicks him. "You are quite the pretty little thing…" he says his voice trailing as he hauls her farther away into the darkness, with Sarah screaming and crying.

"I swear to you. The dog has it. If I had it, I wouldn't let you hurt my friends, you idiot!" I scream again.

"Shut that moron up…will you, Samson?" Abel yells as he keeps dragging Sarah away.

"Please, please!" I scream. "I'll get it from the dog. You come with me. I promise the dog has it. Just let her go!" Abel stops and turns around, still dragging Sarah. He heads back toward us in the little room and shoves Sarah in front of him.

"Well, this is your lucky day pretty girl." Abel chides. Sarah falls to her knees crying. I bend down to comfort her, but get hauled back to my feet by Samson.

"I guess we will have to capture the dog," Samson says.

"Get the bag with the chains," orders Abel to the guy with the bandana… "and get their phones and put them in the backpack."

Samson, Abel and the baseball cap thief start shoving us back further into the room near the trunk at gunpoint. "What could possibly go wrong?" Adam chides me quietly.

"I know…I know…I am sorry. **Magic** will rescue us…You'll see." I reply.

"Shut up you two. I can gag you…no problem," Samson threatens.

We all are quiet, trying to avoid complications. I start praying silently, so afraid for my friends. I got them into this mess. I need to get them out of it.

"Here, take the end of this chain," Abel says to Samson as he hauls a thick, massive chain out of a black, canvas duffel bag. "Wrap the end around the pillar with this hook and, here, Thomas, (the thief with the baseball cap), take this end and wrap and hook it around the other pillar down there." Abel points to the other end of the room. "Chain them at least six feet apart with these hooks on the pillars, Saul, (the guy with the bandana and scar). First bind their hands and feet with this rope." He tosses the rope to Saul. Meanwhile, Jonah holds two guns on us.

"Ouch, take it easy," Jesse whines as Saul binds our hands and feet.

"Make sure they can't get loose. Cinch those chains tight." Abel instructs the others. "We need to get that dog. I don't think it will be hard to find. We know what hotel it's at. One of us should stay and guard these brats."

"I will," volunteers Jonah.

"Oh, yeah," Samson replies. "You are still whining about your hand. What could you do if one of them gets loose? Abel should stay. He's the only one out of all you losers I trust to keep these troublesome teens at bay."

"Oh, like you're the ultimate judge of character," Saul replies.

"I'll stay." Abel says. "Samson is right this time. I will feel better if I am in charge of these moronic teenagers. Just make sure you get the dog. From what I have seen of that dog, it might be tricky to capture it. Keep in touch."

During this whole scene I am doing some serious thinking and praying. *I know God has a plan, but I'm not sure I'm going along with it wholeheartedly. Of course, there is the possibility that God tried to dissuade us from engaging in this caper. I need to pay more attention to signs from God as I would sure hate to be responsible for getting us all killed. It just seemed like we had a good plan. I am surprised these thieves came so prepared. They seem like bumbling fools. God please keep us safe, and forgive me.*

Our only hope is ***Magic.***

CHAPTER TWENTY-THREE
MAGIC REVEALED

Magic races through the allies of Venice. She finds the cathedral where the thieves first hid the amulet, and Paul and his friends discovered what the thieves were up to. The door is ajar and she pushes it open with her nose. In she goes. She starts to puff up and glow, and the place lights up. She spies a little alcove, and she glides to it. Arriving at the alcove, she looks around, still glowing, and glides to the back where she deposits the amulet. She touches it with her nose, and there is a neon yellow flash that radiates in the alcove. The flash subsides, and in its place stands a gargoyle about four feet tall and three feet wide. It is sparkling gold with transparent wings billowing around its body and a head and body like an eagle with a giant hooked beak. It has nasty looking curled golden talons.

Magic, still puffed up and glowing, stands back and looks at the gargoyle. She growls at it, and the gargoyle glows neon yellow as its eyes seem to protrude from its body like fiery red coals. It opens its beak and speaks in a raspy voice, "Be quick… save the children."

Magic turns and races out of the old, broken down cathedral. She transforms into her smaller, non-glowing self by the time she reaches the door. She heads toward St. Mark's Cathedral, bounding through the allies. People stop to watch the beautiful, enormous golden dog on a mission. She arrives at St. Mark's Basilica. She knows Noah will be there today. *Magic* knows everything. She paces back and forth in front of the cathedral. She isn't even interested in chasing birds. She goes back and forth, back and forth. Hours seem to pass. The sun is starting to set and twilight is on the way. The restaurant near the cathedral is crowded with people eating, drinking and listening to the orchestra. Everyone is happy and enjoying the activities at St Mark's Square. *Magic* plops down in front of the cathedral doors and rests her massive golden head on her paws. She is sad and anxious as she knows the boy she's supposed to take care of is in trouble. Suddenly, *Magic* pops up onto her paws because she spies Ruthie and Adino walking toward her.

"Magic!" exclaims Ruthie. "What are you doing here? Did the kids decide to go into the cathedral again? That is odd that they would leave you alone." Ruthie turns to Adino with a quizzical look on her face. "What is going on? Adino, would you go see if the kids are inside? I'll wait here with *Magic.*"

Magic jumps up and stands alert with her tail strait as Adino enters the cathedral. She is not jumping or smiling but is acting very serious. Ruthie bends down to pet her and see if her collar is broken as there is no leash attached to her. "Her collar is still here," Ruth says to herself. *Magic* gazes at Ruthie anxiously. Ruthie studies *Magic's* face and bolts upright and takes a step back.

"Whoa…your eyes are glowing yellow." Ruthie says to *Magic.* "Paul was right. You do glow. Why haven't I seen it before? You didn't want me to see it. Something is wrong. You are trying to tell me."

Ruthie stands up and rushes to the cathedral doors to check for Adino. He comes walking out the doors just as she reaches for the door. "Watch it… watch out." Adino says as he almost rams into her.

"Adino, something is wrong with Paul and his friends." Ruthies says panic stricken. *"Magic* is trying to tell me. Come. Look at her."

"Okay, you should calm down a bit. See if you can get them on his phone." Adino responds as Ruthie races toward *Magic.* Ruthie takes out her phone and tries to ring Paul.

"Look at her eyes," Ruthie says as she bends down to cup *Magic's* head waiting for Paul to pick up. "It went right to voicemail." *Magic* is still standing alert, her tail straight and eyes glowing. "Something must be wrong because Paul knows to pick up immediately!"

"I don't notice her eyes glowing," Adino says as he bends down and pets *Magic's* head.

"Weird," Ruthie says as she looks at Adino and then *Magic.* "Paul always claimed she glowed and no one believed him. I think the kids are in trouble."

Adino says, "I think so too. Why else would she be here by herself and Paul not answer the phone?"

"I'm calling Noah." Ruthie tells Adino. *Magic* starts pacing around anxiously. "Stay here," Ruthie commands *Magic.*

"Hi," Ruthie says into the phone. "I think there is some kind of trouble with the kids." She waits for a response. "I know, I know. But… I think this might be serious because, when Adino and I came out of the Cathedral, *Magic* was parked right in front of the door without any of the kids in sight. They aren't inside the Cathedral either. I'm worried. Where are you? Why don't we meet back at the hotel? Good. See you soon." Ruthie hangs up. "Come on…let's catch a gondola back to the hotel. Noah is meeting us there. He's on his way there already."

"Come on," Adino responds as he grabs *Magic* by the collar. They hurry off toward the gondolas.

"Here comes one," Adino says. "Don't worry. We'll find them. It is an island after all. I wish *Magic* could talk." Ruthie looks at him in a weird way.

"What?" Adino says to Ruthie. Ruthie doesn't reply.

"Hey, watch the dog," the gondola driver says. The gondola is a small one with brightly colored pink and yellow upholstery. The guy driving it looks like a kid.

"Never mind the dog," replies Ruth. "We just need to get across the canal as quickly as possible. Look… in that gondola ahead of us. Isn't that a couple of those creepy looking guys that were in our hotel? I recognize that black and white bandana and the red baseball cap and army jacket. Why are they looking at…..Whoa…*Magic*….What the heck!! Where are you going?"

Magic leaps out of the gondola and puffs up into this giant, gold fur ball, glowing and sparkling as she glides across the churning water of the cannel and launches herself at the gondola with the creepy guys in it, upsetting the gondola and sending everyone into the water. She snatches the gondola driver by his shirt and gently sets him back into the gondola, perfectly dry.

"Magic!" Ruthie yells. The gondola driver is in frenzy and doesn't know what to do. *Magic* gathers the two creepy guys in the water together

in her giant expanded paws and propels them toward the hotel dock and guards them at the dock, waiting for us to get there.

"Go, Go!" Ruthie yells to the driver. "Get to the dog."

"No way!" the driver exclaims. "I'm not going near that dog!"

"He won't hurt you," Ruthie says. "I promise. Those guys must be bad guys. Quick...get us to the dock. Here is your money. Let's go."

Meanwhile, at the dock, the two guys *Magic* has corralled are trying to climb out onto the dock. It is impossible for them to get out because *Magic* has them in a bear hug. Luckily, there aren't any people on the dock. The gondola, which was transporting the creepy guys, takes off in a whirlwind.

"Quick...pull up to the side of the dock." Ruth directs.

"Keep that dog away from me!" yells the boy gondola driver as he tries to keep his composure while docking the gondola.

"Relax," Adino reassures him. "The dog won't hurt you unless you are mean to us or to her, so just let us out here."

Adino and Ruth hop out and run to the end of the dock. "Okay, *Magic*. You can let them go." Ruthie says. *Magic* slowly shrinks to size, and Ruthie and Adino grab the guys and throw them onto the dock.

Adino says, "Can you imagine if our gondola driver had seen *Magic* glowing and engorged?

Ruth smiles at Adino. "You did see!" Ruthie exclaims. Adino smiles.

Adino and Ruth haul the two puny, creepy guys off the dock by their arms and the back of their shirts while they struggle and threaten Ruth and Adino, *Magic* trotting along after. They drag them back along the side of the hotel and throw them up against the wall so as to be out of view. *Magic* stands there in alert and glowing softly.

"What have you done with the kids?" Ruth yells. They both look at each other and don't offer any information. "Well, if you refuse to talk, I'm sure our dog will be more than happy to scare it out of you.

Magic growls, her teeth barred and her fur fluffing up and glowing. The men cower next to the wall.

"I don't know what you're talking about," says the guy with the bandana.

"Yeah, are you crazy?" says the guy with the baseball cap. "You can't manhandle us this way...and keep that psycho dog away from us."

Ruth pulls out her identification which shows she is a detective. "Sorry, I can pull you aside for questioning." Ruth hopes they are too stupid to figure she has no jurisdiction in this country

"We don't know what you are talking about." the guy with the baseball cap says. "Besides, you are a cop in the United States, not here. Back off...both of you and your vicious dog or whatever that thing is." They both push Adino and Ruthie out of the way as they rush off and disappear into the hotel.

"*Magic* is never wrong," says Rutie. "They have something to do with Paul and his friends who are missing. Let's follow them."

Magic takes off running into the hotel with Ruthie and Adino close behind.

Ruth, Adino and *Magic* creep along through the lobby following the two thieves unbeknownst to the thieves. The thieves are leaving puddles of water along the way. "What a couple of morons." Ruth whispers to Adino as they hide behind one of the many pillars in the extravagantly decorated lobby. *Magic* is as quiet as a mouse hiding with them like she is well aware of the hunt. There are many pillars and alcoves furnished with cushy, colorful furniture which makes it easy to hide.

"Stay back," Adino whispers as he holds Ruth's arm. "Did you see that guy? He finally turned around to see if they were being followed."

"Well… you would make quite a detective." Ruth teases as she follows his instruction.

He smiles and says, "Okay, let's go. They are going faster...headed to the elevators. There...that one just closed. Watch where it stops... fourth floor...let's go."

All three jump into the elevator and push the fourth floor button. "Oh my gosh!" Ruth exclaims as they get on the elevator.

"What?" Adino asks.

"That's our floor too." Ruth replies. "Creepy." She whispers. Adino looks at her with his brows furrowed.

The door opens, and Adino holds the door with his hand. Ruth peaks her head out and catches a glimpse of the two creepy dudes ducking into a room with a burst of loud voices.

"Well, aren't they a crafty bunch." Ruth says. "Geeze…haven't they heard of keeping a low profile. I know they are behind the missing kids. *Magic* showed us that. Let's go to our room and tell Noah all we know.

Magic turns and heads straight for their room. Adino and Ruth exchange questioning shrugs.

Chapter Twenty-Four
The Great Escape?

"What the heck!" exclaims Thomas, the guy with the baseball cap as he bursts through the door of their hotel room.

"We're in trouble now!" shouts the guy with the bandana, his voice fading as they enter the room.

"Are you guys nuts?" questions Samson as he jumps up from the gold wing tipped chair almost knocking it over. "Keep your voices down! And why are you all wet?"

Jonah stands up and come towards Saul and Thomas who just blasted into the room.

"Sorry…sorry." Replies Saul quietly. "I'm sorry, but you won't believe what just happened to us."

"Yeah… that is some psycho family." Thomas adds.

"What… what?" Samson questions.

"Well first…we search around the streets throughout the canals," Saul starts explaining. "We don't see hide nor hair of the darn dog anywhere. So we hail a gondola and start across the canal toward our hotel. About half way across the canal, our gondola is attacked by this gold, whirling, fiery fur ball that upsets our gondola, and we go flying into the filthy water of the canal, while somehow the gondola driver ends up in the gondola perfectly dry. It was disgusting….and unbelievable. What the heck is that thing that looks like a dog some of the time and a huge, hideous blur or fireball the rest of the time?"

"And…that's not all." Thomas continues. "As if that wasn't enough of a nightmare, the monster dog, or whatever it is, latches onto us, and we go propelling through the water like a racing boat and almost get slammed into the dock. We try to get out of the grips of this hot, stinky, furry thing but he's got us in a death grasp. Finally, we're being hauled out of the water by these two idiots who drag us to the side of the hotel and throw us up against the wall. Then they start to question us about our whereabouts and the missing teenagers, while the one flashes a badge in our faces."

"Badge?" Samson questions. "What kind of badge?"

"She had a police badge from Los Angeles with 'Detective' written on top."

"Oh that's great." Samson replies. "Way to keep out of sight. Now we have the cops on our tails."

"How were we supposed to know?" Thomas whines. "We didn't notice anyone following us. Besides, she has no jurisdiction here in this country. We told her that and broke away from them and ran like crazy."

"Oh…so you ran like crazy," Jonah repeats. "Where did you run to?"

"Well…here…that's why we burst into the room yelling!" replies Saul.

"That's just brilliant!" exclaims Jonah. "They probably are waiting out in the hall after following you right to your room."

"We aren't that stupid," replies Thomas. "We made sure no one followed us here. We hid in the lobby and waited for a couple of minutes before taking the elevator. Besides, we are soaking wet. Like that isn't going to draw attention and suspicion to us. We had to get out of the public. Who knows who saw those two cops ruffing us up?"

"I better call Abel and tell him this development." Samson says reluctantly. "You two better stay hidden." Samson points to Saul and Thomas. "The two cops won't know we're with you. I'll tell Abel we need to be super careful with the noise level of those teenagers, and, definitely, keep a lookout for that ferocious dog. What a nightmare this is turning into. Those darn kids. Why couldn't they just mind their own business and chase girls?"

Samson takes his phone out to call Abel. "I sure hate to have to make this call." Samson says. "You idiots…why couldn't you just stay hidden?"

"Wait a minute…you're the one who told Thomas and I to search the alleyways." Saul whines.

"We've got a problem," Samson says into the phone……

Chapter Twenty-Five
Hot Pursuit

"Where have you been?" Noah questions Ruth and Adino as they come through the door.

"You are not going to believe what just happened!" exclaims Ruth.

Magic stands alert, glowing with her tail straight as she listens to Adino and Ruth tell Noah what has just transpired.

"What is up with *Magic*?" Noah interrupts before they can even get to the part about *Magic* upsetting the gondola."

"Just wait." Ruth cautions impatiently. "Listen to the complete story. Then you will understand what is up with *Magic.*"

Noah listens intently to the complete madness. He rubs his forehead and takes off his baseball cap and rubs his thick, red hair and says, "Geeze…is this ever gonna stop…I mean…last year we have a confrontation with a monster and now a kidnapping? We have to call the police…and what is up with *Magic*?"

"Can't you see her glowing?" questions Ruth.

"That's why I'm asking about her." responds Noah. "She is all alert and ….like…glowing."

"I know!" exclaims Adino. "We've seen her do amazing things!"

"Why don't we do some investigating on our own first," Ruth suggests. "We don't even know what's going on. The only thing we know is that the kids are not with *Magic*. For all we know, *Magic* could be the one that is lost, or maybe the kids are stuck somewhere, like in one of these abandoned cathedrals. One thing is for sure…Paul is right about *Magic* glowing and being able to transform into an unbelievable supernatural creature!"

"I'm upset that I never believed Paul about *Magic's* transformations and glowing," Noah says sadly.

"Well, what shall we do?" Adino questions in his Greek accent.

Noah looks at Adino and says, "Wow, you sure got more then you bargained for when you hooked up with this family. Honestly, you can leave if you don't want to get involved."

Adino flashes his toothy smile, puts his muscular arm around Ruth and says, "Are you kidding? Ruth thinks I make quite the detective. I wouldn't think of leaving you two alone to figure this out. I'm in for the long haul"

Ruth smiles up at him...all six foot four feet of him.

"I have to say I am happy you are on our side, but you still haven't explained about *Magic* and her so-called supernatural powers." Noah responds.

"Oh, of course, Noah," says Ruth. "You wouldn't believe how *Magic* puffed up and was a fiery glowing gold when she jumped out of the gondola in pursuit of the weirdos in the other gondola...and her speed was unbelievable! When she found us at Saint Mark's Cathedral, she was alert with her tail straight and fur up around her neck and her eyes were glowing gold, just like Paul has always claimed."

"Really?" Noah questions. "I wonder why, up until now, Paul has been the only one able to see her transform? We need to keep this information to ourselves. People might think we're crazy as it is pretty obvious *Magic* only reveals herself to those she chooses. Weird. Maybe that explains how she just magically appeared on Paul's bed when we first found her. What is she? Where did she come from? It is a mystery to me...and why has she not revealed her qualities and powers to us until now? I have many questions. Maybe Paul knows. I know he has tried to tell me on many occasions that *Magic* is a special dog. I just chalked it up to youthful imagination. Boy...was I wrong."

"We were both wrong," Ruth says. "Maybe when we find Paul, he will be able to shed some light on the subject, but... right now... we need to make a plan."

"I think the first thing we should do," Ruth says thoughtfully, "is find out who is really missing, *Magic* or Paul and his friends. But...

those guys we questioned acted very suspicious…and *Magic* was acting ferocious and frantic, which I think means she knows something is wrong."

Adino responds, "There is definitely something shady going on, as *Magic's* transformation was amazing when she wanted to catch those guys. She seemed to be intent on capturing them. Maybe, if we go across the canal…again, *Magic* will lead us to where the kids are, if they are in trouble. That could've been her intention when she met us at the cathedral."

"Good thinking! Exclaims Ruth. "I'm going to make a detective out of you yet."

"Like we need another detective in this group?" Noah exclaims. "So the plan is to go across the canal and turn *Magic* loose?"

"I think that might be the first idea we should pursue," says Ruth. "If she doesn't respond to our request, we will have to search the canals ourselves."

"Let's do it." Noah demands.

Magic yelps and heads for the door. They all exchange curious looks.

"Hail that gondola," shouts Noah as they reach the canal.

"Geez, I hope it's not the ones who saw the whole encounter with *Magic* and those weirdos." Adino says.

"Good," Ruth says. "This guy doesn't look familiar."

"Watch the dog," the gondola driver says.

We all exchange looks, not knowing what to expect from *Magic.* She sits quietly on the floor of the gondola, sniffing the air, glowing slightly.

Chapter Twenty-Six
Change of Plans

I sit crammed up against the cold pillar struggling to try and work my hands out of the chain that binds me. It feels like my hands are wet, so I'm thinking I might be bleeding. *If I could only get loose, I think. I could rush Abel and get the keys from the backpack. But if that didn't work, he might shoot me or the others.* The silence is broken by the ring of Abel's phone, a choo choo sound, of all things. All of us are startled by the sudden break in silence. We all look at each other.

"A detective? Oh…that's just great!" shouts Abel into the phone. "What is wrong with you guys? Do you not know what keeping out of trouble means? It means… don't do things to stand out in the crowd. It seems like you morons are going out of your way to be noticed!" He paces back and forth around us while he listens to the explanation on the phone.

We all exchange looks while I'm silently hoping that the detective they've run into is Aunt Rue.

"Do not move out of that room." Abel shouts again. "Do you understand? Obviously, one of the kid's parents and the darn dog know the kids are missing."

I look at my friends all tied up and scared, and we all make hopeful eye contact again. I silently pray to God that he rescues us and forgives me for dragging all my friends into this.

"What if they go to the police?" Abel questions. "Maybe we should leave the kids here and make a run for it…before they find me holding the kids captive."

Abel listens to the reply on the phone.

"Dogs can sniff their owners out, dummy." Abel sneers. "Haven't you ever heard of how the police use dogs to find lost people? I have an idea. Why don't you guys try to track them down before they find you? There are only two of them, and one of them is a very small woman. You could take them. The dog probably has the amulet or has given it to them. Either way, you have weapons and could take them captive and make them tell us where the amulet is. They probably value their lives more than the amulet. These kids, who think they are junior detectives, will give it up when it comes to their lives or their relative's lives. Besides, the detective lady and her boyfriend might not even know about the amulet. I'm sure the dog can't talk. That would be TOO weird. The teenagers and the dog appear to be the only ones who know about the amulet." Abel gives us a threatening look.

"Well… are you still there?" Abel screams into the phone. "What do you think? Pack our stuff, and get everything ready to leave. We need to get the heck out of here before someone discovers the kidnapped teenagers. We'll be in deep trouble if we get caught. After everything is packed, you, Saul and Thomas go look for the detective, the boyfriend and the dog. Have Jonah take all our stuff down to a water taxi and get it to our car in the parking structure. He should be ready to go when we arrive with the amulet. You three should be able to take on the detective, her boyfriend and dog. Once you find them and retrieve the amulet, come get me. We'll leave the kids here and go meet Jonah at the car and high tail it out of this mess."

"What if you don't get the amulet?" Abel questions the thief on the other end of the phone. Would you rather be arrested for kidnapping and thrown into a jail in a foreign country where they keep you there for life and toss the keys into the canal?" Abel responds sarcastically as he listens intently to the response. "I know that we worked hard to get the amulet." Abel continues. "I hate these kids for snooping around and messing everything up." Abel glares at us and shakes his fist.

"All is not lost….go find them, and let me know what's going on!" Abel orders as he disconnects his phone.

"Change of plans, kids." Abel announces to the teens.

"You'll never get away with this." I say. "You might as well let my friends and I go. Maybe none of us will end up with the amulet. Let us go, and we won't tell anyone that you kidnapped us and stole the amulet and are hiding out here in Venice."

"Yeah… right kid." Abel responds. "Nice try, but I'm going to gag all of you now, so you'll keep your fat mouths shut."

"We've been quiet and cooperative," says Adam. "You don't have to do that. Like Paul says… we'll be quiet. Just go. It's obvious you've run into a glitch… so go… while you still have a chance."

"Shut up…you snot nosed kid. The glitch is your stupid dog." Abel snaps back. "If it weren't for that infernal dog, we wouldn't be here, so pardon me if I don't take your advice."

Abel goes to a backpack and drags out some bandanas. He begins gagging the girls with the rolled up bandana slicing into their mouth. My friends all start yelling and struggling against him. Abel picks up his gun and whacks Micah in the head with the butt of his gun. Micah passes out, and his head just hangs there. Anastasia and Delilah are crying and gagging. Abel threatens them with the same punishment if they don't stop making noise. Both girls quiet down but keep whimpering.

"I am so sorry." I say sincerely to all my friends before he gags me. "I hope you can forgive me for getting us into this mess. Please everyone pray for us and *Magic*."

"You shut up too," snaps Abel. "I've heard about enough out of you meddlesome kids. Why couldn't you just mind your own business?"

Chapter Twenty-Seven
Deliver Us from Evil

Jonah, the thief left in the room, starts throwing all their belongings together while the other three thieves take off chasing Ruth, Adino, and *Magic*, although they are not aware they are chasing three adults and a dog. They are unaware of Noah at this point.

"There they are!" Samson exclaims as they zigzag in and out of the brick alleyways and over the bridges on the canals along the tiny storefronts where all matters of business are taking place. "Who's that with them? Great…they picked up another person." They wind their way through the visiting tourists trying not to draw attention to themselves.

"Let's come up behind them and force them into that abandoned cathedral where we first hid the amulet," Thomas instructs. "it's near hear."

Meanwhile, Ruth, Adino, and Noah follow *Magic* as she too zigzags her way through the alleys and canals of Venice. They act nonchalant so as not to attract attention, even though they are with a giant golden retriever who everyone notices and wants to pet. Their hearts are pounding with the fear of their beloved family and friends facing severe consequences of crossing paths with gangsters.

"There… she went down that ally," Ruth says. They turn down the alley and are suddenly grabbed by their arms with a gun shoved into their backs. They stop and look at each other in surprise and disbelief. "Run, *Magic*!" Ruth screams.

"Don't say another word, detective," Thomas, the wimpy looking thief says.

Surprisingly, *Magic* stops and turns to see her three people being commandeered by the three bullies she's had her eye on. *Magic* starts to growl with a vicious snarl on her face. "Tell that dog to back off or it will be dead in the street." Samson, the massively built thief orders as he shoves his gun into Adino's back.

"It's okay *Magic*." Ruth croons. "We are fine. Let's just do what they want us to. We don't want to get hurt." *Magic* lays down on the brick-paved alley and whines.

"That's more like it." Saul the creepy thief says.

"Keep walking!" Samson orders as he shoves the gun into Adino's back, harder this time. Adino lurches forward and encourages Ruth and Noah to do the same. *Magic* gets up and walks with them.

"There...in there," says Samson with his gun in Adino's back forcing him into the cathedral where they had originally hid the amulet. He shoves his gun into Adino's back. Adino lurches forward.

"Stop that!" shouts Adino who's just as massive and muscular as Samson. "I'm going, I'm going."

"Shut up, if you value your life!" Samson exclaims. He grabs Adino by the arm and shoves him further into the cathedral. *Magic* races in ahead of them and disappears into the darkness. Ruth is silent as she is waiting for *Magic* to do something. She knows *Magic* always comes to the rescue.

"Over here...in this alcove," shouts Samson as he guides Adino through the darkness.

The thieves back the three up against the wall. "Where's that darn dog?" asks Thomas.

"Don't worry about the dog," Saul replies as he holds his gun in the face of Ruth. "We've got what we need right here. Now...just tell me where you hid the amulet, and you can finish your vacation in Venice, and we can get the heck outta here."

"What? Amulet?" questions Ruth. "That is what this whole thing is about? Oh, I get it...You guys are the ones that stole the amulet from King Tut's tomb, and you're hiding out here." She starts laughing.

"Shut up!" screams Samson holding Adino by the arm while he has his gun stuck in Adino's back.. "You won't think it's so funny when you are lying on the ground with a hole in your face!"

"Leave her alone," shouts Adino. "I guess you must be afraid of me, so you pick on the small woman. What a brute you are... you chicken."

"Wait…wait…" Ruth pleads as massive Samson shoves Adino against the wall and holds his gun under his chin.

"We don't have the amulet." Ruth clarifies. "If that is what this is all about, I'm afraid you've got the wrong tourists."

"No we don't," snaps Thomas. "We caught the teenagers trying to steal our amulet, and the dog ran away with it, and we have the kids tied up in another cathedral. We find you with the dog, so, obviously, you and the teenagers are in this together. If you want them to live, I suggest you give us the amulet. Just give it to us, we will leave, and no one will get killed."

"Brilliant!" exclaims Saul, the super creep. "Now you just told them everything. Give us the amulet!"

"We don't know anything about an amulet," Noah responds calmly. "This is the first we've heard of it. Please….take us to the kids, and we will work this out. There is no need for all this violence. You can take the amulet and run. We don't care. The kids will know where it is."

"The stupid dog took it!" exclaims Samson. "Didn't you hear me?"

"The kids will know where she hid it," explains Noah. "Just take us to the kids."

"No way…that's it." Samson shouts. his voice as enormous as he is. "Get your silencer on your gun. We've got to take action."

"Geez!" exclaims Ruth. "You guys are a bunch of bumbling fools, and you expected to pull this off? This is certainly one for the archives."

"Shut up," yells Samson in her face.

Saul reaches into his bag to grab his silencer to muffle the gun shot, and before he can grab it, the entire cathedral lights up with a yellow glow. There is a deafening roar like a lion in an echo chamber that explodes around them. The thieves step back and look around. At the entrance to the alcove, a gigantic, neon yellow flash radiates in front of them. The flash subsides, and in its place is a gargoyle about ten feet tall and five feet wide. It is sparkling gold with transparent wings billowing around its body with a head and body like an eagle. It has nasty looking curled, golden talons and a giant, sharp, hooked beak with fiery red coals for eyes. It's the same gargoyle that *Magic* made from the amulet, only much, much larger.

"What the......!" Samson exclaims…but the gargoyle opens it beak and out shoots an explosion of fireworks. The thieves fall paralyzed to the floor, dropping their guns and lay motionless.

Noah, Ruth and Adino stand there motionless. Their mouths are agape and their feet are frozen to the floor, wondering why they are still standing. There is another neon yellow flash, and the gargoyle shrinks down to its original four feet tall. It stands motionless. Out from its side pops **Magic,** all glowing and anxious.

She runs to them, and they all hug and pet her. She barks at them and turns to go. She wants them to follow her. Ruth says, "Grab the guns, and let's follow **Magic!**" Adino and Noah gingerly pick up the guns. "Give them to me, and I'll put them in my purse, you big babies."

Magic races out of the cathedral with Ruth, Adino and Noah running behind her. Again, they race through the brick alleys trying not to attract suspicion. "I hope **Magic** remembers where they are." Adino says.

Ruth looks at him and says, "**Magic** is no ordinary dog. She knows where to go."

Magic turns and looks at them and barks as she bounds through the streets.

Venice, Italy, Saint Mark's Square

Chapter Twenty-Eight
No Way Out

"Look!" Noah says. "She turned down that alley. We must be close. Stop…we should make a plan."

"Let's catch up to *Magic* first," Ruth whispers. "There she is. *Magic,* come here…come on girl." *Magic* trots back to where Ruth, Adino and Noah are. They all kneel down and pet her. "This is what we will do." Ruth continues whispering. "When *Magic* leads us to the entrance, I want you guys to hang back. I will go in first, gun drawn. If you don't hear anything, follow me in quietly, and we will wait until we hear something…anything that might indicate the kids are here. Then I will creep ahead with *Magic*. She will sniff them out. On the other hand, if you hear me call out after *Magic* and I enter, get the police and wait for them to arrive. Here, take these…" Ruth hands Adino and Noah the guns and silently shows them how to use them. "You won't need them. Keep the safety on and just hold it on whoever we find. Just act like you know what you're doing."

"I don't want to let you go in by yourself," Adino whispers. "It's too dangerous!"

"Dear Adino, I do this for a living." Ruth replies. "Besides, *Magic* will be ahead of me, and she will protect us all. I'm sure they will be hiding in the back somewhere. The worst thing is that we don't know how many of the thieves there are. As I remember, when I saw them in the lobby as we were checking in at the hotel, there were only about five or six of them. We left three of them at the other cathedral passed out, so I'm guessing there couldn't be more than two here."

"I think we should all go in together," suggests Noah.

"Look, it is better for one of us to scope it out first," Ruth whispers. "If we all go in, we're sitting ducks. Please just follow my lead."

"Ok," Noah and Adino agree reluctantly.

"Go on, *Magic*...find Paul," Ruth says to *her* and pats her on the back."

Magic takes off toward the first door of the cathedral, stops and stands at alert, ears perked up, tail straight, and her fur slightly glowing gold.

Ruth opens the door a little very carefully. *Magic* and she duck inside quietly. Nothing. They both wait a minute, and Adino and Noah sneak in too. Ruth touches her finger to her mouth to indicate silence as she crouches down and follows *Magic* who is also crouched down. Noah and Adino creep behind carefully. *Magic* stops and starts to glow slightly and puffs up. Ruth turns and looks at Adino and Seth. Then they hear it……

"Stop your sniveling!" Abel yells at the girls. "Geez, for junior detectives you sure are a sorry lot."

Ruth puts her hand out to keep everyone at bay, while she grabs *Magic's* collar.

"Where can those guys be with the amulet?" Abel complains aloud. "You send dummies to do a job, and that's what you get….a job done dumb. Why aren't they answering their phones?"

Ruth creeps ahead up to the wall of the alcove where Abel is holding the kids. She sees Micah tied to a pillar with a gag in his mouth and blood trickling down his head from a nasty wound by his hairline. She catches his eyes, and they open wide. Ruth puts her finger to her mouth for silence. Micah motions his head to the right as if to show the guy holding them is down the alcove. Ruth peeks around the corner and sees the rest of the kids all tied up and chained to the pillars. But she only sees one of the gang of thieves standing there trying to call up someone on his phone. Ruth enters the alcove, gun drawn and creeps silently toward Abel. She raises her gun and cocks it. Click. Abel freezes at the all too familiar sound of a gun being cocked. He whips around and drops his phone.

Magic stands in front of him all puffed up and glowing with a huge snarl and a horribly vicious growl. "Back off…call that thing off…I don't want to get attacked by that creature."

Nobody does anything to call *Magic* off. She just continues to stand there and growl.

"I'm sorry to break up the party, but I think you've got something of mine." Ruth says. Adino and Noah round the wall and stand there, guns pointed at Abel. "Call the police Noah and keep watch for any of the other thieves that might be here. Adino, ungag the kids." Ruth reaches into the back of Abel's pants and pulls out his gun. "Here Adino." She hands the gun to him. "He won't need this anymore. Frisk him for more weapons when you finish ungagging the kids."

"Give me the keys for the chains, you big bully!" Ruth demands.

"I don't know where the keys are," says Abel. "I didn't chain them up."

"I'll frisk him," Noah replies as he walks back into the alcove. "I've called the police, and they are on their way. I told them there was a kidnapping, and we have the thieves that stole the amulet. There is no one else in this cathedral that I could find."

"He's lying…the keys are in that black backpack." I shout after Adino takes my gag off.

"This looks a lot worse than it is," pleads Abel. "Honestly, I was trying to protect the kids from the other guys in my gang."

"Don't listen to him," I instruct Aunt Ru. "He's lying. He hit Micah in the head with his gun and knocked him out."

Adino retrieves the keys, while Noah frisks Abel.

Adino continues unlocking the kids. "Take one of those chains, and chain this Einstein to one of the pillars, and, by all means, gag him."

"Just stay by your pillar until everyone is undone," instructs Ruth. "We don't want any confusion." *Magic* remains right next to Abel, glowing and puffed up.

"You dumb meddlesome kids!" shouts Abel as he is being dragged to a pillar and chained up.

"Settle down, settle down," Ruth says as she holds the gun to his face. "You sure have a mouth on you…please gag him!"

Adino finishes locking Abel to the pillar and gagging him. Noah gets all the kids unchained. Sarah runs to me and throws her arms around me. I hug her back. She starts crying, and I can only tell her, "I am so sorry to drag you into this."

Sarah responds, "That's okay. We all agreed to be involved. I am just glad you aren't hurt or worse, dead."

Anastasia, Delilah, Adam and Jacob scurry over to Micah to make sure he's okay. I lead Sarah over to Micah and the others. We all hug. My dad, Ruth and Adino join the group hug and Dad says "Thank you God."

"It seems I can't take my eyes off you guys for a minute." My dad teases us.

"What about the other thieves?" I question my dad.

Adino, Aunt Rue and my dad all shake their heads and laugh. "You won't believe it when we tell you," Aunt Rue says.

"Come here, **Magic**," I say. She comes over and we all get down and hug and thank her for rescuing us.

Noah heads out to meet the police to direct them into the cathedral where Abel is chained up.

Magic takes off running after him.

CHAPTER TWENTY-NINE
HEROES AT LARGE

Magic arrives back at the cathedral where the thieves were blasted by the gargoyle. My dad, the officers and I are right behind her. "In there… where we left the other thieves!" My dad shouts to the officers as we run to the entrance. We burst through the gaping door and head to the back alcove. There sits *Magic,* her tail swooshing back and forth as she keeps guard on the downed thieves.

"What happened to them?" I ask my dad.

"You wouldn't believe it if I told you," he answers.

The officers stand and survey the scene as their eyes adjust to the dark. Suddenly, a warm golden glow shines out of *Magic's* mouth. We all look at her. I walk over to her and pet her head as she nudges my hand and drops the missing golden amulet into my hand.

I stand up with a huge smile on my face displaying the golden eagle amulet in my hand.

"That's it," exclaims one officer, "The missing amulet!"

"Is that what this whole thing has been about?" the other officer questions. "You kids are responsible for recovering the stolen amulet?"

I stand there smiling with the amazing, golden glowing amulet in my hand. We all stare at it while the thieves snooze on the floor. *Magic* barks as she stands and wags her tail. *I silently thank God for letting all of this come to a positive end and hope my friends forgive me for getting them into this mess.*

"Can you hold on to that son?" the officer asks me.

"I sure can." I reply smiling as my dad puts his arm around my shoulder grinning at me.

"Does this mean you're not mad at me for getting into this mess?" I ask my dad.

My dad replies, "Well….now…I wouldn't go that far."

The officers are amused. They turn their attention to the thieves who are starting to come around. They whip out their handcuffs and lock them up and hook them together so as to keep them contained.

"You meddlesome kids!" Samson screams. "All our plans shot because you couldn't keep your nose out of our business."

"Move along…move along," the officer directs the thieves as they push them through the cathedral and out onto the alleyway. "You and your son need to follow us to headquarters to give a statement." He says to dad and me.

"Will do," my dad replies.

"I'll take the amulet now," the officer says.

I hand it to him, and it stops glowing. We all look at each other. *I'm thinking, that's weird.*

The officer turns the amulet over in his hand. "I'll be darned. It stopped glowing," he says. He looks at ***Magic*** and me and shakes his head. "Radio ahead to let them know who we're bringing in."

"Al momento," the other officer replies.

All my friends, Aunt Rue and Adino come running up to greet us and make sure we are okay. The thieves give all of us the 'evil eye' and grumble as they are being hauled away in cuffs. The other officer with Abel walks up to join the rest of us, and the thieves all start arguing about whose fault it was they got caught.

"Do you want to come with us to headquarters while Dad and I give our statements?" I ask everyone.

"We've all been informed that we need to give statements," replies Aunt Rue. "They have to be the worst thieves I've ever encountered. We also need to get some medical attention for Micah."

Magic barks and runs ahead to lead the way to the police boats on the canal.

Gold Amulet

Chapter Thirty
"Catturado"

When we come upon *Magic* waiting at the dock next to the police boat, the officer says, "Wait, how did that dog know these were police boats?"

I smile and reply, "She's *Magic!* She is responsible for us catching the thieves. It was her idea all along."

The officer gives me a funny look. I figured maybe he didn't understand what I was saying because I wasn't speaking Italian.

We all pile into the boats that are waiting. They are little black and white motor boats. There are three boats to take us all to the station. The station is painted an orange color and is sitting directly on the water with a walkway to the entrance. It is two stories, and the only entrance I see is from the water.

The officers hustle the thieves out of the police boat, onto the dock and into the station. The thieves' arguing gets louder. "Silenzio!" shouts the arresting officer to the thieves. The thieves quiet down, and another officer comes out and takes the thieves into custody.

"Wait...wait," Samson says before they lead them through the double doors. "What about Jonah?"

Abel says, "Leave it be, Samson."

Samson says, "I will not. There is another one of our group in the parking structure who's gonna get away. That's not fair. He didn't do much as it is. You cops need to go get him. He's driving a navy blue SUV rental on the second level, the fourth space as you hit the level"

Three of the officers take off out the door and hop in a boat and head in the direction of the parking structure.

"Medico," the officer shouts again. The officers lead the thieves through the double doors. *Thanks goodness that is the last I will see of them, I think.*

The station is large with a desk off to the side of the room. The walls are all painted white. It is very plain. The two large double doors lead back to some other part of the building. It looks like a typical government type building like the DMV, except there are colorful tile floors.

Meanwhile everyone is petting ***Magic*** and looking at the amulet the officer is flashing around for everyone to see. "Too bad it stopped glowing," the officer says with his thick accent. "It was the weirdest thing. As soon as Paul here handed me the amulet, it stopped glowing. What do you all make of that?"

We all laughed and pat ***Magic*** on the head. "Hey, like I said, she's ***Magic!*"** I responded. The officer gave us all a curious look.

"Siete gli eroi!" the officer shouts.

All the other officers in the station shout, "Evviva!"

Of course my dad knows some Italian and translates, "You are heroes! Hurrah!"

We high five as ***Magic*** bounces around the station gathering as many hugs and pets as she can.

In comes a nurse who is directed to Micah and the wound on his head. The nurse attends to him with the supplies he has brought. *I am thinking he got hurt because of me.*

A group of people crowd through the door with cameras and microphones. Evidently, it is the local and national newspaper reporters. *I'm thinking it's a good thing the station is large. Are all these people here about us?*

"Which one of you is Paul Wonder?" One reporter with a microphone shouts.

My dad puts his hands on my shoulders and guides me to where the reporter is shouting. "Right here," Dad says.

I motion for all my friends to join me and say, "We all did this together, including ***Magic.***" My dad gathers up all my friends and ***Magic*** and pushes them to the front to be interviewed with me. We are asked a bunch of questions and get accolades and pats on the back and, of course, ***Magic*** makes out like a bandit with pets and praises.

The entire police staff gives each one of my friends and I and *Magic* a certificate of appreciation and bravery. There are many photos taken of us with *Magic* right up front and me holding the amulet. I guess the local and national papers will have us in the headlines. We are also informed that the government of Egypt will be in contact with us and a monetary reward will be in store for us as well.

"It's a good thing you guys are heroes," my dad says, "because my boss would've had my head on a platter for this escapade after the fiasco we went through last year in Scotland."

"Amen!" Aunt Rue says.

"Ruff, ruff!" *Magic* responds.

CHAPTER THIRTY-ONE
BACK TO ROME –
WHEN IN ROME.....

We all are bittersweet about leaving Venice, Italy. It is a cool place. It is well worth exploring, but we are glad to be getting away from those nightmare thieves. The limo taking us back to Rome, Italy is really cool. The Italian government upgrades it to accommodate our entire group comfortably. They want all us kids to ride together back to Rome.

All of us are busily chatting about how inept the thieves were. They were like bumbling fools. We can't imagine how they managed to steal the amulet and make it as far as Venice without getting caught. Abel, the one guarding us, was a little guy with a big mouth and evil spirit. Samson was like a giant with massive strength. He would've snapped my leg off if I hadn't relented. Sarah was brave and courageous. We all agree on that. *I think that it was my entire fault she was almost hurt by Abel.* I put my arm around her and give her a squeeze. She smiles at me.

Sarah says, "I think we all owe our lives to **Magic.** She is the one who saved us and captured the thieves. What an awesome and special dog she is." **Magic** sits up and everyone pets and hugs her. I see her start to glow. I look at Sarah, and she smiles and says, "I see too."

"Dad," I say. "Remember how King Tut's tomb is rumored to have a curse on it? Maybe that was the reason the amulet was out to get those guys. When we held it, it just glowed, but it burned and threatened them."

"You have a good point, Paul." Dad replies. "It certainly is food for thought."

"Along with how the amulet turned into a gargoyle and blasted fireworks at the thieves." Aunt Rue says nonchalantly.

"Wait, what?" We all question

"Whoa….back up." I say. "What do you mean a gargoyle and fireworks?"

"Oh that," Aunt Rue says as she winks at Adino and flashes a smile at Dad.

"We'll save that account for dinner conversation tonight," Aunt Rue says smiling.

"Well..all is well that ends well, thanks to **Magic**," dad says.

"What does that even mean?" I say *thinking to myself…why does dad always say that. My mom used to too and what is this about the gargoyle and fireworks.*

My dad chuckles and says, "Everything worked out. That's all it means. I have to say that the Lord was certainly watching over you guys these past few days. It reminds me of John 14:27 (NIV). Jesus tells his disciples: 'Do not let your hearts be troubled and do not be afraid.' I am just wondering what you guys were thinking when you set out on this venture. Your hearts were troubled over the thieves, but you showed amazing courage in the face of terrible danger. You acted in a way that showed me Jesus was with you the entire time, protecting you and guiding you as you showed such courage and conviction in your actions. I am really proud of all of you and am glad that I am on this trip with such an amazing group of people." He high fives us all and we all whoop.

When we all settle down, I say, "I can honestly say that I was praying the entire time, I prayed for courage and that my friends would forgive me for getting them into this entire mess."

Everyone chuckles and starts throwing things at me, saying "Yeah… you almost got us killed, and we are never listening to you again, and what were you thinking?"

"You can forget me ever allowing you to venture off on your own again." Aunt Rue says as she throws her map at me.

"Aw…..come on Ruthie," whines Micah. "I've been injured, so can't you ease up a bit and let us explore Rome when we get there?"

"Over my dead body!" Aunt Rue exclaims.

Magic barks. "I don't want to hear anything out of you**, Magic**," Aunt Rue responds as she hugs **Magic.**

"By the way, Dad," I say, "What did your boss say about this whole fiasco?"

My dad takes his baseball cap off and rubs his hair while he looks distressed. "She was not very pleased that her children were kidnapped and almost killed….but she was very pleased with all of your bravery in even pursuing this caper. She also claimed that it would be good publicity for our company. She did mention that she might rethink having kids come on trips with their parents, since it was two years in a row that bizarre incidents happened.

"I can assure you Ruth that we have all had enough adventure for one trip," Sarah replies. "You should feel free to hook up with Adino for our last few days."

"Yeah, we can't forget about 'lover boy'." I tease.

"Well… lover boy was quite instrumental in us finding you." Aunt Rue replies. "And he may have quite the recollection of the gargoyle incident."

"Okay, let's remember how blessed we are to be together all safe and sound," Dad says. "When we get to Rome, there will be enough daytime left to do some exploring. I believe I will let you kids go off on your own for a few hours, IF you promise to just check out ruins and eat gelato and pizza. No jumping in fountains or following suspicious people, and, above all, do not let *Magic* out of your sight! We have a few more days in Rome, so plan your time wisely.

We are all amped up and noisy, and Jacob says, "When in Rome….."

"Don't tell me we're back to that again." Dad says.

"Come on," Dad says, "I want to have a prayer before we end this limo ride. This is the best time since we are all together and venturing off on another adventure….this one I hope is less treacherous then the last."

We all join hands and bow our heads, and *Magic* puts her paw on my sneaker and her chin on my knee.

"Dear Heavenly Father…."

Rome Italy, Trevi Fountain

www.ingramcontent.com/pod-product-compliance
Lightning Source LLC
Chambersburg PA
CBHW030435120726
47903CB00003B/980